Sex and Candy

This evening, there is nothing but this: soft chocolate breasts inside my strong hands, roll and pinch of skin, my fingers lathered in Macy's dew and sweat and sweet cream. There is only her reaching, dark fingers, hungry mouth.

Inside my mouth she is the first spoonful of tapioca pudding. She is finding a fudgesicle in the freezer on a hot summer day. She is the sweet cinnamon bloom of apple pie up on the tongue. She is the perfect cake, hot from the oven.

I fuck her the way others perform surgery. Abrupt. Precise. Focused. As though each kiss is a breath of air, each slip of tongue is a sustenance and fruit.

Also edited by Rachel Kramer Bussel:

Naughty Spanking Stories from A to Z
Naughty Spanking Stories from A to Z, Volume 2

Sex and Candy
Sugar Erotica

Edited by Rachel Kramer Bussel
Foreword by Shar Rednour

Sex and Candy

Cover Design: Eliza Castle

First Pretty Things Press Edition 2008

First Printing 2008

ISBN: 157612-299-9

Manufactured in the United States of America
Published by Pretty Things Press

987654321

To Candy Lovers and Sugar Freaks everywhere.
—RKB

Foreword

Rachel Kramer Bussel *is* candy. Like my mom always said about dessert, as long as you eat right at dinner you definitely deserve her. I bet you bought this book because you know that you deserve dessert. I'm sure that Rachel's readers are the one audience that doesn't require my lecture on the importance of indulgence. That's what I love about you! These stories will certainly leave your body shuddering to the urgent pulse only a sugar rush delivers.

I first became friends with Rachel over my book *Starfucker* (out of print, but search the web because it's priceless and nasty). Her story about Monica Lewinsky is as indulgent as they come. I didn't know back then she would turn into the Cupcake Queen, but now it all seems so obvious. Sugar whores always come out of the crystalline closet sometime. Usually with dirty knees and licking the icing from their lips. And little did she know back then that I would put my sugar fantasies on tape in my movie *Sugar High Glitter City.*

The general plot reads as, "*Sugar High Glitter City* is a futuristic sexcapade that ushers the comeback of the (never existent) '70s dykesexploitation genre. Sugar is outlawed and cane-addicted dykes stop at nothing to get it, even selling their own bodies."

This idea had been swirling in my mind for several months, but it really cooked up to softball stage, as we say in fudge-making kitchens, in the red velour interior of our van "Rosita" on the way home from the "Porn Oscars," the AVN Awards in Las Vegas, where our movie *Hard Love & How to Fuck in High Heels* had won Best All-Girl Feature. We had really gone there to party with our fabulous San Francisco-freaky cast of stud butches and babe-alicious femmes. The porn world exists on the fringe of society and we queerly sashayed down their red carpet as the fringe of the fringe. My wife and co-producer, Jackie, and I had indulged in a particularly great, never-ending three-way that weekend with only-seen-in-the-movies mirrors on the ceiling and a gigantic bathtub in the bedroom that we kept filled with bubbles and surrounded by candles. We each took our turn crawling away from the lust pleasure in the bed to have a glass of champagne and a respite in the tub. A moment of relaxing alone in the flickering glow while sounds of sex—maybe kisses, maybe post-orgasmic moans, maybe intense, demanding urges—filled one's ears, beautiful bodies provided eye-love and warm calming water nurtured one's pussy for round 4 or 5 or 12.

Legendary writer Michelle Tea and her poet-stud Rocco had come along for the ride, the party and the story (she wrote the cover story "Boogie Dykes" for the *San Francisco Bay Guardian*). As we raced home through the desert, all reliving the crazy weekend with gossipy tidbits about everyone there and, of course, repeating the moments up to our win over and over from each person's angle, Michelle, I think it was, asked, being the good journalist, "What would we be doing next?" Jackie or I told of a few ideas we had been toying with including the sweet-themed flick. Oh did Rocco ever jump on that one. And that's all that I need. Jackie, too. Someone to (Cadbury) egg us on in our altered reality. Rocco was a sugar freak, too. Confessions, I love confessions. And soon everyone in Rosita was brainstorming all of our scenes. Rocco wrote a poem for it soon after. We kept feeding off of each other and literally getting whipped into a sweet cream frenzy.

I went home and worked on my script. I showed it to Jackie and  she smiled kindly, too kindly, with disapproval as she stood up from the computer. "Honey, I never thought I would be the one to say this but, *it's just a porn*. It's times like these that *that* phrase comes up." I gasped and she continued, "You've written a wonderful plot and created over-the-top characters, but it's like a five night miniseries." She paused, my ever-fuckable critic, "A five night miniseries for people who care as much about sugar as you do . . ." which was to imply that not everyone did. "And don't get me wrong," she added pulling my hips from behind, "you know I love a miniseries."

So I chopped off the anti-heroine The Salt Queen who'd have been lit in low blue light in her cool white cave. She kept her slave-boi chained to a salt lick when he wasn't licking her pussy—I had already researched the only farm supply store that sold salt-licks online and now I'd have to let that go. Salt was the other vice orig-

inally in *Glitter City*. Believe me, I think food is only a waste of calo-
ries unless it is used as a vehicle for salt, so all the salt sex was going
to be good.

I chopped off how the Army funneled money into *Glitter City*
through a politician (who, of course, gets done every which-a-way).
There was gonna be dykes getting fucked with sugar canes begging
to suck them off. Just confessing all this to you is making me want
to make the sequel.

We made *Sugar High Glitter City* with its cut down plot, and we
had a blast doing so. We ate sugar, pussy, dyke-dick and more. I was
in hog heaven every time I called out to my props manager to "bring
on the sugar." She would jump between the naked bodies to plant
lollipops, straws of colored sugar,
hard candy bites, gum drops, and
any confections she could find in
SF. Although we ate lots of candy
and had lots of orgasms, Jackie
and I had plenty of leftovers—
baggies of brightly-hued treats,
not just candy but flavored con-
doms, that we gave away at par-
ties. Soon *Sugar High* got picked
up by Frameline's SF LGBT film
festival, and thereafter any festival
daring enough to show explicit
erotica picked it up as well. Our
candied cocks and cunts shown
around the world. Then we got invited to speak at universities about
FEMINIST PORN. Whether it was there or at the Q&A after theatre
screenings, we always got asked what inspired this movie? No one
asked that about *Hard Love & How to Fuck in High Heels.* Isn't it odd
that a movie so obviously titled and featuring sweets would be
questioned as to its "real plot." What was it *really* about? Drugs???
For the record, Rachel never needed to ask what the movie was *really*
about. And neither did thousands of other sugar freak sluts around
the world, thank you very much. But many did. The non-believers.
It is about women owning their own bodies, but all of our movies
are, and about the definitions of legality. What is illegal and what is
legal and how absurd the lines are dividing the legit and the underground.

But as to the original seed of inspiration? I never tell. All of our dyke movies come from real turn-ons, and in our educational line from the real gut-driven desire to show folks exactly how to do something they want to try to do.

The original seed. Or shall I say grain? The original grain of sugar that fed us our most popular movie? My desire to pleasure Jackie.

To explain, you'll need to know that I am pretty much a hardcore dyke. There have been a couple of guys that have turned my head as opposed to thousands of women. And one of the aspects of being a lesbian that really appealed to me was that I would never need to give a blow job. I thought of giving a blow job as inherently submissive and unappealing. I had plenty of straight women friends and gay men who loved doing it and I supported them on that but for me it was not up my alley. At all. And  since I was not motivated by loving or lusting after a bio-dick toting human there was never a natural instigator for me to explore or learn more about sucking cock. Well then, as lesbian sex oceans have want to do, the sappho tide changed where sucking off a dyke-dick became the latest trend. Many butches, especially, but some other lesbians, too—and this is before "transman" was even a word but obviously transmen-to-be—confessed how they loved or fantasized about getting a blow job. Oh, blow job, blow job, blow job! I had helped women find their G-spots, shown them how to fist, and explored SM as much as the next gal, but now this trend is just ridiculous, I thought.

But there was Jackie, my love. And I hate to disappoint. So I figured out a way that mouthing her wand would appeal to me too. Because me really wanting to do it was part of her fantasy (many folks wouldn't have had that requirement, wink, wink). We were both sex educators, after all. I was very familiar with teaching men and women about condoms—how different ones functioned and which ones were the best quality, etc. Good Vibrations had multiple bins of every kind of responsible condom sold. I loved thrusting my hand into the bins of the candy-colored flavored condoms and fingering their slick wrappers, squishing the ring I could feel inside.

The one that was the bright Bubble Yum shade of grape purple caught my eye the most. And the fuschia one. Rich, intense colors that I associated with hard candy or gumballs. I told Jackie that if she made her dick candy I might be motivated to crawl across the floor for it. Faster that you can get to the center of a Tootsie Pop, she not only had a bucket of flavored rubbers at home, but she had gotten her baby some other inspirational treats as well. She held up lollipops and gummy treats and sour strips, too. Sugar Pimp was born and her candy ho delivered all the right licks.

Back to my mommy, she also always said, "We *have to have* dessert," after every meal. Not so much a command but a statement of the obvious in her sing-song voice. Simply saying the near future out loud, because even saying it set the enjoyment in motion as she cut a piece of pie if we dined at home, or dug in her purse for a Lifesaver if we'd eaten on the go. Sex and sweets we indulge in for pleasure of it all. Sugar is the *perfect* prostitute—you pay your money, she honestly loves you for those moments, gets you high, and leaves you blissful as she tiptoes out. In your foggy hangover, you see a love letter on the nightstand. Here it is: *Sex And Candy*.

Yours in Glitter & Confection,
Shar Rednour

Introduction: Sugar Rush

Sweet. Creamy. Gooey. Luscious. If you ask me, sex and candy have a lot in common. Both can make us lose our minds a little, getting into a frenzy where all we care about is tasting it, swallowing it, having it that very moment. Sex and candy make us reckless, wanton, hungry, horny. As Michele Zipp puts it, "The desire for candy as a child is like the lust for sex as an adult. It's craved, it satiates, it even calms." For me, quite often, sugar makes me ravenous for someone else to share its sweetness with, or at least, makes me want to lick someone else after I've gotten done licking the frosting off a cupcake, savoring a Kit Kat or Nestle Crunch, or devouring a smooth soft-serve ice cream cone on a blazingly hot day.

When publisher Alison Tyler asked me if I'd like to make my dream of a sugar erotica collection come true, I was actually sitting in my favorite bakery, sugar Sweet sunshine on Manhattan's Lower East Side, enjoying a delicious vanilla cupcake. I often go there on weekends to write and people watch, and sometimes I don't even need to sample their delicious treats to absorb the thrill of being surrounded by sugar. The air simply sings with it, and I think that's the reason I've witnessed many people heading there while on a date (though I do often satisfy my craving for a cupcake or slice of crumbly, cinnamon-and-sugar-emblazoned coffee cake).

Sugar is sensual, and when we indulge in it, we really do indulge. I've never been one for raisins in my salad or pears in my main course; I firmly believe that dessert is for dessert. I like to take my time when I eat sweets, giving them the proper attention they deserve, kind of like sex. I don't love quickies because I'd rather roll around in bed all day, or for as long as I can, going back for more and more and more. I like to savor a mouthful of ice cream, letting the creamy goodness slide along my tongue and down my throat. I like to suck on candy canes for as long as I can, savoring that sweetly spicy taste. I love dipping my finger into a bowl of cookie dough batter, tasting the tang of salt and sugar and the occasional chocolate chip. And, surprise surprise, all of these treats make my whole body ache. When I'm alone, indulging my sweet tooth, I always long for a lover to come and kiss his way down my back, his tongue making me melt just like the sugar disappears on my tongue. I long for a gorgeous woman to part my legs and lick me to ecstasy as the sugar soars in my bloodstream. A surefire way to make me melt is to bake for me or simply offer me a sweet treat, preferably consumed directly from your fingertips. Maybe it's because I have a decided oral fixation, but I'm certainly glad I'm not the only one.

In the scrumptious stories collected in this book, you'll read about everything from Turkish Delight to cinnamon rolls, pudding to cotton candy, taffy to Twizzlers. These tales are funny and quirky, sensual and tasty. Some are the equivalent of slowly savoring a lollipop or peppermint stick, sucking and sucking until your tongue turns colors. Others are the kind you want to gobble down immediately—the candy bar that you can't wait until you get home to try, or the ice cream of SékouWrites's "TimeReleaseDessert," melting

before you've had a chance to truly savor it, making you need to eat it in a hurry. The authors here have gone all out in their quest to show you just how much pleasure can be wrung out of some "Old-Fashioned Fudge." They take you all the way to Italy for delicious gelato and to New York for Magnolia Bakery's famed cupcakes —but Stan Kent's story would've been way too racy for *Sex and the City*. I can guarantee that you'll never look at a luscious, shiny candy apple in quite the same way after reading Radclyffe's sizzling "Cinnamon Secrets." Sacchi Green's protagonist in "Sugar on Snow" gets asked a vexing question: "Which would you prefer, ravishment or eating?" but these lusty guys and girls know that you can have your dessert and get eaten, too—in fact, they excel at wooing their lovers with sugary delights.

Donna George Storey opens *Sex and Candy* with her fabulously sensual, exquisite "Six Layers of Sweetness" that will arouse and move you, making you yearn to peel back the layers of your desire—and to ask her to make you a Venetian. Then enjoy the guided tour through all manner of candy, baked goods, chocolate, and a few surprises, concluding with my personal favorite, the cupcake, which appears twice, in Jolene Hui's "Banana Afternoon" and Stan Kent's closer entitled, simply "Cupcake," the word itself a naughty double entendre (if you've ever said to someone, "I'd like to taste your cupcakes," you'll immediately see what I mean).

To me, sex and candy are two of life's most perfect delights. Combining them, whether you're feeding your lover a bit of brownie, getting beaten with a big lollipop, licking ice cream off someone's chest, smearing frosting all over yourself, or teasing someone by sucking suggestively on a popsicle, can truly make your head spin.

I suggest settling down with some of your favorite candy or sweets, whatever they may be—this is a book meant to both satisfy and whet your appetites, and I'm pretty sure you'll finish each story even hungrier, and hornier, than you were when you started.

Rachel Kramer Bussel

Six Layers of Sweetness
by Donna George Storey

Michael laughed when she said she'd bring dessert—a low velvety sound that made Laura think of sex.

Then again, these days almost everything made her think of sex.

As she buttered the sheet cake pans she used for her special Venetian cookies—the ones she made when she wanted to impress someone—Laura realized that tomorrow night she would not only be thinking about sex, she would likely be having it, with Michael.

That is, of course, if he passed the six-layer test.

And that required much more than a deep, sexy laugh.

Laura measured the flour and salt into the sifter. An invitation to dinner at his place, an offhand mention Jason would be with his mom—even a woman as rusty at dating as she was could figure out that a little mattress dancing was on the agenda before the evening was through. She hadn't been to his house yet, but she imagined a bedroom done up in browns and tans—safe "guy" colors—and bland Scandinavian furniture. He'd have a king-size bed. Divorced men needed king-size beds to stage all of their requisite post-marital-trauma acting out. And on that bed she saw a woman—herself—lying as cool and chaste as a marble figure on a tomb as Michael knelt beside her to unbutton her blouse. Even in her fantasy, he did not bend to kiss her breasts once he'd uncovered them. He merely gazed as if dumbstruck by awe. Or fear.

Laura sighed. Michael had been such a gentleman since they started seeing each other outside of Computer Committee meetings at the school almost four weeks ago. A perfect gentleman, respectful and kind.

She hoped to hell he had some juice in him somewhere.

She took a can of almond paste from the cupboard, a brand she ordered specially from a gourmet catalog, and spooned out eight ounces onto the kitchen scale, then tipped it into the food processor. This was her own inspired addition to a recipe she'd begged from a Dutch friend almost a decade before. It made the almond paste light and feathery, no lumps to weigh down the tiny cake layers, so delicate they rose no more than a quarter-inch high. She must have baked these cookies dozens of times over the years, and she'd assembled a long list of tricks to ensure success. Still there was always a pang of doubt when she set about on a new batch. Could she perform her sorcery yet again—take ordinary flour and butter and eggs and make them into something transcendent?

Making Venetians was rather like making love (ah, yes, sex again, what they said about randy widows was too true). Much of it was routine, a predictable intertwining of limbs and naughty pink parts. Some was hard-earned skill: her late husband Ernst had dubbed her tongue tricks better than Viagra. Yet in spite of years of experience, disaster lay in wait for any slip, a single moment of complacency or inattention. Two years ago, at Christmas, she'd ruined a whole batch, all three pans turned a sooty black for no reason she could fathom. Of course, that was right after Ernst's fatal heart attack. Everything around her had turned to black.

Now, the April evening lingered gold and pink outside the kitchen window. Laura felt her face relax into a smile as she began creaming the butter, the European kind with extra butterfat. This was the easy part, familiar as taking your husband's cock between your lips as you stroked him, just behind the balls, to bring forth that delectable little groan. Slowly she shook in the sugar, spring snow melting quickly on the fluffy, pale yellow mountains of batter. Next came the four egg yolks and a teaspoon of almond extract, colorless but surprisingly potent, filling the kitchen with the scent of an almond grove in bloom. Yes, she had done this dozens of times.

Suddenly she winced at a new pang of doubt. Perhaps Michael didn't like almonds. She hadn't thought to ask. Ernst had been very fond of her Venetians, and she'd been proud to earn compliments from a man raised on Vienna's finest pastries. But Michael wasn't Ernst; there was no mistaking one for the other. Ernst had been lean and wiry, with a silver lion's mane, every inch the eccentric professor of education and psychology. Michael was stocky, his hair still a burnished gold. His hands had the sturdy competence of a man comfortable tinkering with computers—and other mysterious, delicate things. That's how they met, when he volunteered to head the Computer Committee at the school, a lifesaver for Laura who'd reluctantly taken the faculty advisory role after so many years of avoiding it. Michael ran things quite smoothly, in spite of his youth. He was only thirty-two. At forty-two, Laura was the same age as Ernst when they were married, a world-weary Austrian and his twenty-something bride.

They were indeed such different men and yet she wanted the

same thing from them. All she had to do was close her eyes to feel it, hot and hard, pushing her open so quietly, with no sound of all but a soft suck of juices. Not like the buzzing ice-blue vibrator that had been her sole consolation for too many months.

The Venetians, she hoped, would change that.

Oddly enough, she'd used cookies to seduce Ernst, too. Brownies, actually, baked from scratch with cocoa imported from Holland, a bold step for a girl raised on cake mixes and Cool Whip.

Looking back, Laura was amazed at her own audacity, the innocent arrogance with which she'd plotted her conquest. She was convinced on the slimmest evidence—a warm smile, a gaze that lingered at her perky breasts or her tight buttocks just a few beats longer than it should—that the professor was hers if she wanted him. After all, a fresh twenty-two-year-old girl was a prize any middle-aged man would find irresistible. Mere sweetness was enough. She had to believe this, because sweetness was all she had to offer.

Ernst would be a prize for her as well, of course. To fuck a man almost old enough to be her father, she thought, would be like drinking his formidable power into her body, stealing it away from him, from the whole masculine world. This wasn't true either. Laura had learned that lesson well enough. Yet she had been right about something else—her sense that Ernst would savor her, not like lovers her own age who seemed to gobble her up as if they were afraid she'd turned back into a wet dream.

The brownies had only been part of her arsenal. Laura had spent hours shopping for lingerie before she settled on a garter belt, not the predictable black lace kind, but a dove-gray beauty, embroidered with tiny pink roses. It was imported from Europe and reminded her of the handiwork of nuns. She paired it with crimson lace panties—in the language of lingerie she'd basically scrawled "fuck me" across her ass in blinking neon. She covered it with a flounced peasant skirt and danced over to his cottage at the edge of campus and offered him her tray of brownies with a wiggle of her hips. "Would you like to try some, Professor? They're still warm."

The words didn't come quite so easily as he made love to her for the first time in the cool light of the fading winter afternoon. His kisses tasted of chocolate and the coffee he'd served with a gracious smile, but soon Ernst put his lips to other uses, and one in particular that surprised her.

Talk.

First he praised the eloquence of her skin, flushing blossoms of arousal against the soft, pale meadow of her chest. Wouldn't she open her eyes and gaze upon its beauty? She must watch his fingers as they tweaked and twisted her coral nipples into stiff, little knobs? No need to hide in darkness, he'd switch on the lamp so she could see better, see the faint trembling of her belly as he stroked it, the shiver in her thighs as he nudged them open. Of course she must look as his finger made its novice explorations of her most tender parts. She must tell him if he was doing it right. Was it the right place? It wasn't too hard? He would wait for her expert instructions now . . . should he continue?

Laura could barely croak a yes—yes, please—for she was indeed trembling with desire and shame at the scene before her, her own body transformed by the alchemy of his hands and words. Propped up on fluffy pillows against his headboard—like a queen, he said—it took every ounce of will to keep her eyes open, to look down on her own flesh as she had never seen it before. Pink blotches dotted her breasts like the alphabet of some foreign tongue proclaiming her desire. Her lush, hairy mons looked all the more brazen against the nuns' delicate stitchery. The rosy crescent of her swollen inner lips strained toward release around Ernst's slender, busy fingers. Laura's nostrils prickled almost painfully with the scent of her own juices: fruit mixed with spices. Her ears, too, felt newly opened, assaulted by the sound of her own gasps, her choked pleas yielding to his soothing reassurances. No, she mustn't hold back and wait for him to be inside, he wanted her to enjoy a climax right now. He wanted them both to watch—open your eyes now, Laura, you can do it—to watch the most beautiful vision in all the world, a woman at the height of pleasure. There would be another chance, very, very soon, for them to share in the same, but for now she would not deny him this singular sweetness.

She did not. She shrieked like a witch as she came, her body jerking, none of it beautiful at all, she supposed, but Ernst's soft gray eyes, meeting hers, pressing into her, filling her. She had never felt her desire so exposed, pink, raw, glistening. She had never felt her pleasure as such a presence in her body—sound, sight and sensation swirling and melding into a magic potion that bubbled, stretched, and finally, exploded inside her so that all was lightness and air.

Laura switched off the mixer and tested the egg whites. The beaters left twin mounds with soft, ice-cream-cone swirls at each tip. On a whim, she pinched one off with her fingers. Perfect. The rest of the work she would do by hand, folding in the flour and salt, then the egg whites. Dividing the batter into three equal portions and coloring one green, one pink and leaving the other a creamy, virgin hue.

That was another problem with the whole thing, of course. Ernst had been such a fantastic fuck, a real scholar of every sensual delight. It had been one of the reasons he loved her Venetians so well— six layers of sweetness, he called them. He made a sacrament out of savoring each nibble.

And what of Michael?

She had hopes for him. Even her daughter Colette had picked up on it. Just yesterday, she'd studied her mother with her wise, gray Ernst-eyes, unnerving in a twelve-year old. No doubt, she'd guessed why her mother had suggested a sleepover at Lily's on Friday.

"When do I get to meet this Michael?"

"When I figure out whether I like him or not."

"Oh, you like him. You always blush when you talk to him on the phone. You're even blushing now."

But he hasn't passed the real test, she wanted to answer. The six layers. Each part was simple enough, except the last. Until then, it was all foamy fantasy, meringue without sweet flavor. Until she knew, she wouldn't even burden her daughter with an introduction.

She wanted Michael to do well. He certainly seemed to enjoy his food, a promising sign for an interest in other appetites. But what if they didn't fit together right? He was a big man, but what if his cock was tiny or, worse yet, monstrously huge? She'd had a boyfriend like that long ago, a shy fellow with a thick purple truncheon of a dick tucked away in his jeans, and she had to limp around for days afterwards, groaning aloud whenever she bent to sit down. Maybe that was the reason for Michael's caution? He was divorced, after all—everyone had past sorrows beyond a certain age—but was there a good reason for it? He might be the kind who thought women needed it rough and a few cursory pawings at the breast counted as enough foreplay to plunge inside, his full, muscular buttocks pumping away to the rhythm of his own pleasure. His poor wife would have tired of that after a while. Or he might have a different problem with timing. She pictured him kneeling between her legs, poised to enter her, then erupting in helpless spurts of jism, spraying her belly and thatch with hot white cream, one stray shot reaching her nipple where it beaded there like a pearl.

Even that sorry vision made Laura tingle *down there*.

She wiped her brow—lust, not a hot flash, she hoped—and began to measure out the pink batter into the first oblong cake pan, smoothing it even with an offset spatula. Then she rapped the pan on the table, three sharp whacks like a spanking, to get the air bubbles out. Only then did she indulge herself in a few cat-like licks of the pink batter clinging to the spatula. It was silly, but each color tasted a bit different, the pink a touch fruitier, the green faintly spiced, and the white more purely almond.

She knew it was all in her head.

Her hands were trembling.

This was one of the most nerve-wracking parts, of course, the first point at which it could all go terribly wrong. If she left the layers in the oven one moment too long, they would be tough and brown, ruined. But if she pulled them out too soon, they would break apart when they came out of the pan and what could have been ethereal magic would be nothing more than wet, gummy blobs of garbage. Laura sat at her kitchen table, twisting her hands as she stared at the oven door.

And there—had her sex-craziness progressed to plain old insanity?—she saw Michael's face, as it looked across the table in a half-dozen restaurants, handsome and smiling.

Have faith, he said, though his lips weren't moving at all.

Laura's second foray into battle, twenty years after her first, called for more subtle weapons: matching panties and bra in pale lilac, a slim skirt and sweater. Just a touch of makeup. Plenty of moisturizer to smooth out the lines. She carried the Venetians in a small, oblong tin. She'd brought a mere dozen one-inch squares so as not to overwhelm Michael. A small sampling of her wares was plenty for a first timer.

The rest of the baking had gone as she hoped, no disasters. The cake layers were light and moist and glided easily onto the filling of apricot jam, warmed and strained until it was smooth as a dream. After an overnight beauty rest came the final touch, a thin coating of bittersweet chocolate.

The right man would declare them absolute perfection.

From the moment she stepped through his door, Laura was pleased at her own sense of ease. Gone were the doubts. (Did her tits sag too much for a younger man? Was the courtly treatment a sign he saw her as a mother figure and nothing more?) She moved through his house, taking in the bland, masculine furnishings that were just as she'd imagined, smiling at the whiff of fabric softener on his shirt and the streaks of comb in his wheat-colored hair. His cheeks were faintly flushed, as if he were nervous about what was to come. In that she had the advantage over him for she knew they would fuck, and as much as it was in her power, it would be very, very good.

But first she sat perched on a stool at the kitchen bar with a glass of Pinot Noir, watching him slice red peppers into perfect match-sized strips for the salad. How nimble and tireless his fingers were.

Michael caught her staring. "I really enjoy cooking. I like doing things with my hands."

"Oh, really?" she said sweetly. How long would it take to get through salad, roasted vegetable lasagne—and damn, he'd mentioned a cheese course, too—before she could feed her real hunger?

Suddenly, he was beside her, an eagerness in his grin that fueled her hope. "May I take a peek at dessert?" He gestured to the tin.

"Of course."

The test had begun.

His amber eyes widened. "Wow," he said. "Did you really make these? How do you eat something so exquisite?"

She laughed. "Just bite into it. That's the polite way. Or you could pull it apart with your fingers and savor each layer one by one. Nudge the chocolate off with your tongue and lick the filling gently from the cake. Like an Oreo. Sometimes I do it that way. I'm not sure if it's childish or very decadent."

"Definitely decadent." He gave her a sidelong glance. "Would I get in trouble if I tried one now, before I had my good food?"

The secret muscles deep in her belly fluttered. "We can do as we like. We're grownups."

His eyebrows lifted. "I suppose I'll try the civilized way first.

I'm still trying to impress you and the other way sounds messy."

She was about to argue that a man who didn't mind getting his fingers wet and sticky would impress her more than anything, but he had already taken his first taste.

She watched his face. His eyes closed for a moment and he made a small, soft sound. Then he didn't say anything at all. He only gazed at her until she had to stifle a moan of pleasure and surprise. His eyes filled her first—the naked longing, the flickers of his own X-rated fancies—pooling low in her abdomen, opening her. Her panties were already wet. She reached for him, hooking an arm around his shoulders. He came and stood before her.

The first layer peeled away.

He made the sound again as he opened his lips to her tongue. She tasted the cookie in his mouth, the almond, apricot and chocolate mixed with his saliva.

The second layer melted in the kiss.

Her fingers itched to feel his cock, but even she had to let the layers unfold in their own time. Instead she pulled off her own sweater, conscious of his eyes falling to her bra, settling on the discs of her nipples visible through the sheer fabric. He moved to unsnap her with a small, serious frown, and though she was in the midst of unbuttoning his shirt, the better to stroke his soft, broad chest, she didn't mind his impatience to take a nipple in his mouth and work the other between his fingers. She was glad he was hungry, too. She arched her back and sighed as he licked away the third layer with low moans of delight.

At last she allowed herself to touch him through his trousers, a nice firm handful he was, thick, like his fingers, but not so long he would hurt her. She eased the zipper open and stroked him.

"We should move some place more comfortable," he whispered.

"No."

His shoulders stiffened with disappointment at her rejection.

"I want to do it here," she added quickly. "Like this."

Out of the corner of her eye, she checked for evidence of fastidious or distaste. What good was a nice, meaty cock if he wasn't willing to be at all creative with it? But it only took an instant for her suggestion to sink in.

Michael yanked her skirt up to her waist as he murmured in her ear, "What a bad example you are to the class, Ms. Mueller, begging a man to fuck you on a kitchen stool."

Layer four, stripped away, consumed, and thoroughly savored.

"I'm not the one who ate dessert before dinner. That, young man, might earn you a spanking."

Grinning, he set to work unbuckling his belt, but paused.

"The condom? Don't worry. I've got one here in my purse."

"If I didn't know better, I'd think you'd planned this."

She raised her ass from the leather seat and pulled at her panty-hose. "Stop thinking so much and help me off with these things. They're soaking."

He made an appreciative grunt as he fingered the crotch of her underwear nested inside the hose, slid them over her thighs and tossed them to the floor. Through lust-hazed eyes she watched him tear open the condom wrapper and roll it over his tool, watched him hunch down a bit as he guided himself into her body. She breathed out, spreading her legs as far as she could around the stool, a deep stretch that tightened her pussy muscles deliciously around him.

Five layers gone and all that was left was the chocolate, moist with bits of almond cake and melted fruit.

Michael resumed his attentions to her breasts, tugging with his lips, twisting with his fingers. Laura reached down to finger her clit, but soon she felt another hand beside hers, waiting, learning, and in fact, Michael did do a very creditable job when his finger took over for hers, jiggling away in just the right spot as she bucked against him. His trousers had fallen to his knees, and she grabbed his ass, raking her fingers across the clenched cheeks, urging him on with gentle slaps, then wilder smacks as her orgasm roared up from the dark, glittering cave where it lay waiting, always waiting, for the right touch to blaze into flame.

She couldn't quite say when the last layer melted away. Perhaps it was when she screamed his name, for it was Michael who was fill-ing her now, Michael who had passed the test with a hunger to match hers. Perhaps it was when he released his spunk into her, the leather of the stool seat squeaking in shocked protest at the vigor of his thrusts. Or maybe it was after he'd mopped himself up and but-toned his fly, and he took her in his arms and whispered, "By the way, I think I forgot to mention that your cookies are the most amaz-ing dessert I've ever eaten in my life."

Then he laughed, low and soft, and she did, too, and the sounds twined together in sweet layers of harmony.

It made her think of sex.

Turkish Delight
by L. Elise Bland

It was the worst candy I had ever tasted—quite a disappointment after I had waited all my life to experience it. I first heard of the supposedly addictive candy in C. S. Lewis' fantasy book, *The Lion, the Witch, and the Wardrobe,* in which an evil queen tempts a young boy with boxes upon boxes of enchanted candy called Turkish Delight. Anyone who tasted it would go on eating more and more of it, even if it killed him.

When I first read the book, I had no idea what Turkish Delight was. The name always stuck in my mind, though, because it was such a perfect sounding name for a magical food, with the "Turkish" part of it conjuring up vague images of genies, magic carpets, and people who wear shoes that curl up into a point at the toe.

Unfortunately, the flavor did not match its reputation. Instead of being irresistible, it was more like one of those old-fashioned candies that people ate before they learned how to make chocolate or anything that actually tasted good. It is a chewy, jellied sweet flavored with rosewater and, if you're lucky, nuts to break up the gummy texture.

By chance one day, I found my Turkish Delight on the counter of a Middle Eastern deli. There it was, resting under a glass dome in all its glory, a stack of sturdy little cubes dusted with a heavy coating of powdered sugar. Behind the glass pastry case stood an even more delectable type of sweet.

"You like to try?" the dark-haired sales clerk asked me. "No charge for you." His name tag read: "Faris." His heavy accent screamed: "Just arrived in the U.S. and searching for a nice American girlfriend." I was ready to apply for the job. After all, I was unattached and had endured a long dry spell. Unfortunately, subtlety was not one of my stronger traits. With my chest out, hair tousled, and lips moistened, I was poised to seduce.

"So, Faris, where are you from?" I asked. "I couldn't help but notice your accent."

"Lebanon, originally. And *your* accent?"

"Kentucky," I answered. I leaned over the counter, making sure he caught a good eyeful of cleavage. "If you're Lebanese, why are you selling Turkish Delight?"

With a wink, he pulled out a piece and presented it to me between a tanned finger and thumb. I couldn't resist. A hottie was offering me free candy—the candy of my dreams, in fact. Instead of taking it with my hand, I took the coquettish route; I parted my lips and he lowered the foreign nugget onto my tongue, just lightly enough to tease me with its intense sweetness.

"This is a very famous dessert from Turkey," he explained. "But we eat it everywhere in the Arab world. We call it lokum."

"So, can I lick your lokum?" I asked, making a stupid joke that didn't work in any language, including my own. Luckily Faris's English was limited. He stared at me with piercing eyes and elegant black eyebrows. I wasn't sure if he was confused, intrigued, or just plain irritated.

"Yes, you will like my lokum. Go ahead." he said. "Eat."

First, I licked off all the sugar, making sure to look into his eyes with porn-starlet hunger. Then I grabbed his wrist, and once I had secured the cube firmly in my mouth, I flicked my tongue along the underside of his fingers. My oral message came through loud and clear.

"I see you like my candy," he said, leaning over the counter, his white apron pressing hard into the glass on the other side. "What is your name?" I couldn't answer him because my teeth were suddenly glued together. I waved my hand before my mouth to distract him from my awkward facial expressions. The candy of my dreams had turned into a nightmare. It had morphed into a wad of tough gelatin that tasted more like medicine than confection. "Spit or swallow?" I asked myself as I chewed with about as much grace as a dog eating peanut butter. I had two choices: either gulp down the bizarre goo and make some extremely unattractive grimaces in front of my foreign object of lust, or I could spit it out, most likely insulting his homeland along the way.

Although my candy seduction had taken a bad turn, I was determined to maintain my composure. It was time for some fancy "TV cooking show" style mastication—the type of staged eating where a glamorous hostess chews with her mouth completely closed, all the while making cooing noises and orgasmic facial expressions for the camera. Eating this candy would definitely require advanced acting skills. But it was too little, too late.

"You don't like? Here. Taste again," he insisted. Reluctantly, I tried a nibble from a different brand and it was just as foul. What a disappointment. Maybe my enchanted candy simply didn't exist.

"I'm sorry," I said, wrapping up the rest of the candy in a napkin. "You're pretty tasty, but your Turkish Delight sucks."

"You are throwing my gift away? You Americans don't understand flavor. There's more to it. You take it with coffee and you'll like it, " he said. "Come with me and I'll teach you Arab food."

"If you can make me like this nasty candy," I promised. "Then I'll find an all-American delight for you to try, and believe me, it will be just as much of a challenge."

"Deal. Meet me tonight. It's late already, but we can taste coffee and sweets. There's music and dancing."

I rushed home to take a quick beauty nap before my late date. After brushing the pink rosewater gelatin out of my teeth, I curled up in bed with my dog-eared copy of the C.S. Lewis book. I skipped straight to the scene where the Queen seduces the young boy with her enchanted Turkish Delight.

As bad as that candy tasted, reading about it still excited me. It sounded completely irresistible, but I sure wasn't anywhere near addicted to what I had just eaten. Nevertheless, the Turkish Delight hadn't lost its charm. Fantasies coursed through my mind and body: evil queens, horny boys, magic potions, taboo candy, hot late-night dates, exotic sex, and foreign tongues. I was supposed to be taking a nap, but I couldn't sleep. My naughty hand soon found the familiar path that led straight into my panties. I was already soaking wet with swollen lips that were aching for a kiss. My fingers whirled around my clit and dug deep into my pussy. The harder I fucked myself, the stronger I felt. I was regal, just like the evil Snow Queen, ordering my addicted servant boy to lick me, eat my pussy, suck my toes, bite my nipples, and then, with the hardest cock possible, fuck me.

Would he let me tie him up? Would he talk dirty to me in a foreign language? Of course he would. Did he have a hairy chest? Foreskin? Would his come taste better than his candy? I could only hope so.

I lay on my back, pressing into the hardest part of my softness, imagining my candy boy as triplets—one cock in my mouth, one in my pussy, and one straight up my ass. I would be filled to the brim with Turkish Delight. I wanted to come, but I held back for as long as I could. I didn't want the fantasy to be over, but ultimately the decision was not mine to make. The phone rang.

"Hello," I answered, panting.

"Hi, it's Faris," he said. "Sorry I'm early. I'm outside in your parking lot. Can I see you now?" I jumped out of bed, and threw on my skirt and top, panties still wet from all the solo foreplay. I knew I was in big trouble. It is always a bad idea to go on a first date without having at least five orgasms beforehand. I didn't want to come off as a loose American woman, but that's precisely what I felt like on that night. I was way too horny to go out in public, especially with a man I hardly knew. I was starving to death. I would eat him alive. I needed to be locked up like a rabid animal, but there was no way I was canceling my date when I could at least get some good action. I was sick of my dirty books and my expensive, faceless toys. I wanted the real thing and I was determined to get it.

Faris came to the door decked out in black pants, a white cotton tunic, and a striped, multi-colored vest. In his hand was an enormous box of Turkish Delight.

"For you," he said. "One day you'll want them."

"Gee, thanks." I took the candy, figuring I'd give it to some unfortunate elderly relative for Christmas.

The restaurant was not the chintzy, touristy kind that so often appeals to Americans in search of exotica, but rather an underground, family-style hole-in-the-wall on the outskirts of town. It was simply called Abdo's, and just as Faris had promised, there was a lively after-hours party going on. When the kitchen closed, the lounge opened up for innocent vices: smoking flavored tobacco, drinking strong coffee, drumming, and dancing to modern Egyptian pop music. It was packed full of people who dressed mostly in American clothes, but preferred not to speak my language. The women sat on one side of the room and the men on the other. The sexes seemed to separate naturally and stayed separate except during the debke line dancing. Since I didn't quite fit in with the Arabic-speaking women, and since it

would have been completely inappropriate for me to sit at a table of only men, I hung out with my hot date in the corner. We ordered a sheesha pipe, coffee, and a sampling of several sweets the restaurant had baked earlier.

Along with lokum, they served other well-known Middle Eastern desserts—Balorieh, which is shredded phyllo dough with rosewater and pistachios, Namoura cakes, Baklava, Borma with Cashew, Bird's Nest Pistachio, Bazarek covered in sesame seeds, and Fingers Cashew. "It's addicting," he said about the final item we tasted, the flaky cashew-flavored "finger." It surely was, all of it. The more honeyed desserts I ate, the more bitter coffee I craved. And between stimulating bites and sips, I took tokes of apple-flavored tobacco from the Alice-in-Wonderland hookah. The balance of flavors was intoxicating and intense, like bittersweet chocolate with dried fruit. It suddenly all made sense—fruity, bitter, floral, and sweet tastes all coming together like a good bottle of wine. I ate so much and so feverishly, I dropped a dusting of crumbs, flakes, nuts, and powdered sugar into my cleavage. Faris saw it, but pretended not to notice. I brushed it off with flamboyance, making a show of my breasts that were all puffed up in my push-up bra. Still, he wouldn't look.

"Are you ready for Turkish Delight?" Faris asked. "You know you have to have some."

"Sure," I said, rubbing his strong thigh. "Bring it on." At that point, he could talk me into just about anything, but for some reason, he didn't. Why hadn't he tried to make a move on me yet? By then, I was about to explode, especially after getting so revved up on caffeine and sugar, not to mention all the masturbation before our date. I was ready for action and he was practically ignoring me.

Two more tiny cups of black coffee arrived along with a plate of lokum. This time, when taken with the coffee, the candy was softer and more delicate. I could actually chew it, and it didn't seem so foreign anymore, especially after everything else Faris had offered me. It passed easily across my lips. It was almost good. Almost.

"Eat sweetly and speak sweetly," Faris said. "It's an old Turkish saying." I leaned over to kiss his sugary mouth, but he shoved me away. "Not here. It's very strict."

"It sure doesn't seem strict. These folks are going wild," I said. I pointed to the floor where people were dancing, clapping, drumming, and shouting in foreign languages. "Let's join in," I said, pulling him up to dance in the debke line. At least that way, I would get to hold his hand, and hopefully more. I had to get closer to him and dancing seemed like it was the easiest way.

He already knew all the steps. I followed along the best I could, but I soon lost my footing and was messing up the line. I tore Faris away to dance with me one-on-one instead. After all, I considered myself a good dancer. But since I didn't know any Middle Eastern dances, I resorted to what I did best—the booty bounce, the butt-fuck move, and the leg grind. In no time, I was practically dry-humping Faris on the dance floor, rubbing my breasts up and down his chest, and even slapping my own ass. The conservative Middle Easterners stopped their debke line and backed away to watch in horror as the American tramp made a total spectacle of herself.

Faris grabbed my wrist and muttered something in Arabic to the crowd. They all nodded their heads politely and he yanked me out of the lounge. We ended up in the dark kitchen that still smelled of the nut-and-honey pastries baked earlier in the day.

"Are you crazy?" he asked me, almost angrily, but with a gentle voice.

"Sorry. It was just all the caffeine and sugar," I paused. "Plus, being with you. I got too excited. If you want me to behave, then just don't feed me anymore of that weird candy. Don't you know it's magic?" I grabbed Faris's thick hair and kissed him. He did indeed have sweet Turkish Delight breath. Finally, I got to taste the real thing. I pulled his body tight against mine and felt his cock pressing up into my belly. Without speaking, he lifted my shirt, knocking a condom loose from my bra. I was busted.

"What if somebody comes in?" I asked him.

"Don't worry," he said. "They won't disturb us. After what I told them out there, they think we're fighting."

"So does that mean I can scream?"

And scream I did. Faris threw me back onto the cold metal kitchen table and crawled on top of me, pulling my skirt up and digging his hard cock into my panties. We kissed for as long as we could stand, and then I shoved him off me so I could undress. I heard the distinct sound of a condom wrapper ripping. "Not yet," I said. "You have to taste me first." I leaned back, naked, in the dark, waiting for what I hoped would be good sex. After my experience with the hyped-up Arab candy, I was a bit apprehensive. But as they say, there's no such thing as bad sex. Or is that bad publicity?

Faris didn't disappoint. He ate each and every sugary crumb off my breasts, then moved down to my pussy where he lingered, inhaling all my aromas. When he finally started to lick, I realized he was a true gourmand. The way he devoured me made me feel like an intoxicating dessert. I lifted my body into his face so he could get his fill.

"Finger me, too, Faris," I whispered. "If you want to fuck me for real, you have to show me what you can do with both your mouth and your hands." He filled my order. He moved two agile fingers in and out of my pussy and sucked on my clit so hard that I arched my back and impaled his hand, shooting his fingers even deeper inside me. We shook and rocked back and forth so much that we sent a metal tray full of Balorieh clanging onto the floor. For a second, I worried about the strangers in the next room, but his lips kept me on track. In no time, warm, strong vibrations sped from my heart all the way down to my thighs. His touch was kinetic, like a jolt of lightning. I let out a series of uncontrollable cries and slammed my palm against the table. He pulled his hand away and buried his face inside my lips, accepting all my contractions and drinking up every last drop of my queenly potion. I had him under my spell, or was it the other way around? I was still shivering from the orgasm when I felt his body on top of me again.

"Was that good?" he asked, kissing me with Turkish Delight and pussy still on his breath.

"God, yes!" I said. "Shukran!" (*Thank you*, in Arabic)

"Did I earn all of you?"

"Go for it," I told him, still in mid-orgasm. "Make me scream like that again, and you can have anything you want." I didn't really get to see his body that night since it was so dark, but I had no complaints. Faris was a natural athlete, the type of guy who knows exactly how to move at exactly the right time. While his hands and mouth were talented, his cock was even better; it filled me up in a way that only a flesh-and-blood cock could. Although I had known him for just a few hours, he seemed to know my body without any training at all. He teased me with his rhythms, which were decidedly different from the Western-style "one, two, three, four" fucking pace. Inside me, he drummed out traditional beats interspersed with strange counter percussions that drove me absolutely wild. I could hardly keep up with his energy. My temperature shot up higher and higher until sweat was pouring down my temples, neck, and back. If he hadn't had such a good hold on me, I would have slid right off the metal table like the pastry tray had earlier.

Faris tore into me at warp speed. I was almost scared of the orgasms that would ensue, so I grabbed hold of the sides of the table to brace myself. I knew I'd have bruises on my back the next day, but I didn't care. I cried out once more as I felt myself plummeting down into a long, dark tunnel that led straight to the magical world of tantalizing sugar and sex. I don't know exactly at what point he came, but he started to scream crazy-sounding things in Arabic and then got very quiet.

After we had composed ourselves, we yelled at each other for good measure and banged around a couple of pots and pans to make it sound like we were really having a knock-down drag-out fight. Then Faris shuffled me out the front door. I kept my head lowered in feigned shame as if I were a wayward woman who had just been chastised in the kitchen.

Needless to say, Faris never took me back to Abdo's restaurant, but we had plenty of fun running around town otherwise. Although I never fell completely in love with the real Turkish Delight, we indulged in each other, savoring each morsel, until the box of enchanted Turkish Delight ran out.

Cinnamon Secrets
by Radclyffe

I smelled her first.

A sweet, spicy scent that cut straight through the miasma of odors that were so familiar I didn't notice them any longer—popcorn, cotton candy, and roasted peanuts. This was a playful, seductive aroma that captured my attention like a whisper of hot breath in my ear. Seeking the source, I gave the metal spike tethering the tent line one more hearty smack with my sledgehammer, then turned around and rested the broad iron head on the ground between my legs. The thick wooden handle nestled against my crotch.

She was standing just behind me, studying me as if I were one of the sideshow attractions, a quizzical look on her face as her dark eyes swept me from head to toe. Her nose wrinkled just the tiniest bit, creasing her otherwise flawless olive-skinned face with an expression not of condescension, but concentration. Her frank appraisal caught me off guard, and I felt myself blushing, wondering how I looked to her in my work boots, threadbare jeans, and sweat-stained sleeveless T-shirt that I'd ripped down the front a couple of inches for ventilation. I wasn't used to women cruising me quite so openly—at least not in a hell of a long time.

I wasn't wearing a bra, and though I'm not particularly endowed, when I felt my nipples tense under her continued scrutiny, I was sure she noticed. Even on a sultry August night in the middle of a dusty fairground, though, *she* looked as cool as a cucumber in one of those flimsy flowery things that my mother used to call sundresses. Her smooth, tanned legs were bare, her red painted toenails peeked through open-toed sandals, and, incongruously, she had a small white daisy tucked behind her left ear. Her shoulder-length ebony hair was pulled back and tied with a pale yellow scarf, and all in all, she looked as if she should be sitting on a veranda on a Bayou plantation a hundred years ago. I smelled that little bit of sin again and watched her take a bite of a big red candy apple.

"Hi," I said, watching her perfect white teeth chisel two matching crescents in the shiny scarlet surface. Juice oozed from the hard white meat inside and little flakes of the candy shell melted on her full lips, deepening them to a moist fiery crimson.

I felt a twinge inside my jeans. Jesus, I was getting hard.

"I know this sounds ridiculous," she said, "but don't I know you from somewhere?"

I didn't answer because I was watching the tip of her tongue snake out and catch the tiny droplets of cinnamon and apple before they slithered down her chin. It was so unconscious, so natural, I couldn't help but imagine just exactly how it would feel if she licked the juice from my—

"I'm so sorry," she said stiffly, her face flaming, "I have no idea why I said—"

"No, wait," I blurted out when she started to walk away. "You do. Know me. I mean, you've seen me. At least, I've seen you." I stopped, realizing that I sounded like an idiot. And I held out my hand and told her my name. "I'm an EMT. You've seen me in the ER. You work the night shift at County, right?"

"Of course!" She smiled, absently sucking at a few streaks of red liquid candy that had dribbled onto the back of her hand. "Without the uniform, I didn't place you at first. I'm . . . "

"Christy . . . I know." Boy, did I know. Every time we transported a patient to her ER at night, I noticed her. She looked great even in scrubs—tight little butt, high full breasts, and long, long legs. I didn't think she'd ever noticed me, though. Usually she was too busy getting report or triaging to do more than toss me a glance. At least that's what I'd always thought. The fact that she had paid me enough attention to recognize me now made me feel good. Better than good. It made me pleasantly horny, just a nice little buzz between my thighs. Unconsciously, I rocked my hips, and when the handle of the hammer bumped my clit, it zinged a bit harder.

"So, you're volunteering here?" Christy asked, indicating the tent with the red cross stenciled on the side.

"Yeah." I grinned. Inanely probably, but she had a fabulous mouth which was at the moment nibbling at the edges of that candy-coated apple. I couldn't take my eyes off the way she licked at it. Every little swipe of her tongue shot right to my crotch.

She looked me right in the eye, turned the apple to a new spot, and took another bite. "I love these things," she said after she swallowed and tongued her lips again. "But I always make a mess." She raised her hand to show the wooden stick that speared the core of the apple. Rivulets of thick ruby syrup trailed down onto her fingers. "I'm going to have to find some place to wash up."

"Come to the equipment trailer," I said. "We've got a john."

"You sure?"

"Yes." Boldly, I held out my hand for her free one. "Come on. It's around back behind the tent."

I led her through the maze of tent ropes, trash barrels, and empty benches to the small trailer that housed the emergency medical equipment and our personal gear. I was the only one on shift at the moment, so we were alone when we stepped into the dim compartment. I switched on the light over the small sink, which gave us just enough illumination to see each other by. The space was crowded, and when I turned back to where she stood just inside the door, we were so close I could feel her breath on my neck. It tingled with the taste of cinnamon. I didn't move. Neither did she. Not until she leaned back against the inside of the door and held up the apple.

"Want a bite?"

Oh, man, did I ever. I slid one step closer until my thighs just grazed hers, braced my hands on the doorjamb on either side of her shoulders, and leaned my head down. "Hold it still," I said.

"Okay." Christy settled her free hand on my hip. "Go ahead. But no hands—just your mouth."

With my eyes locked on hers, I slowly opened my mouth, pressed my lower body a little harder against her, and bit down on the rim of the apple where she'd last taken a bite. My bottom lip brushed the wet surface of the fruit as my teeth scraped over the stiff covering. I closed my lips ever so slowly, edging my hips forward at the same speed until my crotch settled into the V between her thighs. I gave my head a little shake and broke off a section. I ended up with a portion of it extending beyond my lips.

"That's an awfully big piece." Her voice was breathy, and she reached around to my ass and squeezed. "You should share."

I kept the sweet-tart fruity concoction between my teeth and let her pull the other half into her mouth. Our lips met, the candy apple joining us, and we both sucked on it. My head was getting light from not breathing, and the steady rush of blood into my clit was making it ache. I could feel her nipples like small stones crushed against mine. Finally I bit through my half and she sucked the other part into her mouth. I swallowed it fast; so did she. Then our mouths were fused again, free of everything but the taste of cinnamon and sex.

I heard a thump, but my tongue was in her mouth, chasing after the juice and the spice, and I didn't register what it was. I got one hand between us and clasped her breast. She was swollen and heavy in my palm, and when I flicked her nipple, she moaned. The sound made me want to come. Christy pulled her mouth away and held up her empty hand between us.

"Still a mess."

She was breathing fast, her breasts rising and falling with each uneven gasp. My stomach was in knots, my clit like a rock, and there was no way I was letting her move. I shifted my hand from her breast to her wrist and pulled her fingers into my mouth, sucking the melted candy from her skin. Her eyes glazed as she tilted her head back against the door, watching me lick her through half-lowered lids. Her fingertips played over my tongue and as I slid up and down the length of her fingers. I worked my thigh between hers and she rode me to the same slow rhythm as my mouth on her flesh. When her fingers were clean I went after her mouth again, releasing her wrist and dropping my hand to the outside of her thigh. I slipped my fingers under the light cotton dress as my tongue probed her mouth for the taste of cinnamon. She bit my lips like I was her candy apple.

The silk between her thighs was soaked. I traced a furrow in the thin material with my fingertip, slow-stroking the bump of her clitoris each time I passed. Her fist opened and closed on my ass, picking up speed as she pushed harder and harder against my hand. My palm was slippery with her juice. I edged her panties aside. She was swollen and wet, full and ripe—her scent as sweet and mouthwatering as the candy-coated apple that lay abandoned on the floor between us. I fondled her, teasing inside her opening and then up and down her slick cleft, flicking her clit with each pass, until I felt her legs stiffen and her back arch. Then I stopped.

"No, noo," she groaned, grabbing my wrist and squeezing her legs around my hand. "I'm almost coming. Rub my clit, baby . . . baby, rub it nice."

I skimmed inside her mouth, then sucked her lips, gathering the last little bit of cinnamon on my tongue. Then I slid to my knees and pushed her dress up at the same time. I pulled her panties aside and closed my mouth on her sex, working her clit in and out between my lips. She shuddered and whimpered, and then I licked her, catching her drops on my tongue and teasing the essence from her pouting lips. This time, when her clit turned rocklike beneath my tongue, I didn't stop. I circled the tip, flicked the shaft back and forth, and tugged it deeper and deeper into my mouth as I slid two, then three fingers inside her.

"Fuck me," she whispered. "Fuck me. Suck me suck me, do it hard. I'm gonna come."

I looked up at her face as I worked her clit, thrusting my fingers slow and deep, watching her head roll from side to side against the door. Eyes closed, she dug her fingers spasmodically into my shoulders and chanted over and over, "That's it that's it I'm coming, I'm coming …you're making me come…"

I tasted the rush of her orgasm, sweet and rich, just before she jerked against my face. She tightened down around my fingers, releasing a single high cry of pleasure and surprise. She rode my hand and my face, coming hard. I shook uncontrollably with the pressure in my belly, and I jammed one hand between my legs, rolling my clit between the folds of rough denim.

I shot off, doubled over, shivering through my orgasm with my forehead cradled against her trembling thighs. When I could finally focus, I saw the apple lying on the floor between my knees, the sweet red candy melting in the heat.

Every time I've made love to her since, I've tasted the sweet cinnamon secret she saves just for me.

TimeReleaseDessert
by SékouWrites

At two-forty in the afternoon, the man gets up from his desk, opens the office door he always keeps closed and walks to the freight elevator used by messengers because he is less likely to run into co-workers there.

He works as a copy editor for a dessert magazine on the tenth floor of a midtown Manhattan office building, his window facing Radio City Music Hall and overlooking an intersection that swells to capacity every afternoon at lunchtime. He usually tilts his chair enough to watch the river of people flowing by on the streets below him like a stream of syrup, pedestrians seeming to eddy in front of restaurant orifices, trickling in empty-handed and spilling out again with plastic bags, paper cups lanced with straws and handheld Styrofoam containers. True to the avoidance tactics he practices in life and love, he always waits until late in the afternoon to slip out of his office in search of sustenance long after the congested canal of lunch seekers has reduced itself to a tiny tributary.

At a fountain half a block from his office building, he waits for inspiration. In a city of so many food options, his mind is often short-circuited by indecision. As he stares into the undulating ripples of the fountain, close enough to feel the mist from the water tingling into his hands and face, a scent drifts into his consciousness. Something sweet and pungent, redolent of cured meat marinated in bourbon and basted with brown sugar. Seeking its source, he turns in a circle and the smell becomes momentarily stronger before it diminishes, like it's passing him by. His stomach groans, urging him to discover its source and partake of it. Eyes clenched, the man takes a few steps—dangerous in the city of so many fast moving people with short fuses—and hopes for success.

He finds the fragrance and his stomach rumbles as he turns toward it. Opening his eyes, he expects to see one of the ubiquitous metal food carts that materialize at first light to service pedestrians for breakfast and then vanish by the time nine-to-fivers are taking lunch. Already fishing for his wallet, he is surprised to find himself looking into the face of a striking woman instead. Long and lean, her skin radiates sun-drenched hues. Above an amused smile, her wide, dark eyes are studying him with intensity.

"Why are your eyes closed?" she asks.

He knows immediately that she is a recent transplant to the city of concrete and mortar. A seasoned New Yorker would have given any man walking with his eyes closed a wide berth, just in case he proved to be dangerously crazy—as opposed to just crazy. And even if they stopped to watch him (doubtful), the very last thing they would do is engage him in conversation. There is an innocence that hovers around her like a halo of hope. It takes just a moment for him to be drawn so deeply into her that his sense of space, time and equilibrium begin to diminish, as if he is being wrapped in a sweet but mind-numbing cocoon of cotton candy.

"You smell like food," he blurts out.

It is a stupid thing to say, but somehow his attraction for her and his salivary glands are conspiring against him and that's all he can think of. "Food" isn't the word he should have used. It does little to convey the magnificence of his olfactory experience.

Long accustomed to the acerbic behavior of New Yorkers, he expects the middle one of her long fingers to bisect his perspective of her at any moment, but what he gets is a fuller smile, her cheeks pulling up into knots, like small nuggets of taffy. Definitely not a New Yorker.

"I smell like food," she says, rolling the phrase around as if she doesn't believe him in the slightest but is fascinated by the concept. "Well, A for originality, I guess."

She shakes her head and laughs before folding her arms across her chest. Looking at her posture, her smile, the way she is inclining her head, he realizes that he is being graded on his presumed efforts to pick her up. Distracted as he is, he does not want to dissuade her. Recovering, he digs for a business card as she watches him, looking like she is already phrasing how she will relate this odd Manhattan encounter to her girlfriends. He finally pulls a single, faded business card out of his back pocket. His only one.

"Can I buy you dessert?" he asks, matching her smile with one of his own. He has no skills in this arena but knows enough from TV sitcoms that an overture to a future meeting is required.

"Dessert," she repeats with a lingering question mark in her voice. "You're an off-the-beaten-path kind of guy, aren't you?"

"Is that a good thing?"

"I'll let you know."

She turns and walks away without warning, her curiosity apparently in search of new inspiration. Motionless, he watches her—her body's juxtaposition of svelte form and generous curves holding his attention and seeming to cut a ribbon of color through the usual gray that colors his perspective. As he continues to stare, his hunger grows, and he knows there is nothing that will satisfy his appetite now. Except her.

His feet react to her rapid disappearance first, forcing him to give chase in a cautious, meandering way. He tries to stay hidden as she darts from one trendy store to the next. The way she explores the city, taking in each of her experiences with obvious enthusiasm, he becomes even more certain that she is new to the strange world of New York City living. Despite his singular focus on her, it isn't until he sees an older woman stop and compliment some aspect of her style that he realizes his quarry's clothes are fashionable and unique.

As she exits The Gap, he slips close enough to catch the scent of her again and is immediately rewarded, the aroma filling his nostrils, tickling his taste buds and tormenting his belly. He is thrilled to have his senses overloaded by her. The eye candy of her appearance together with the olfactory candy of her smell is an overwhelming combination. He longs to add the sense of touch and, more important, taste to his range of experiences with her.

After an hour of delirious stalking, he spurs himself to action. Catching up easily, he touches her, hesitant, as she is about to enter a fast food restaurant. Short on wit but heavy on desire, he keeps it simple by renewing his offer of dessert.

"What do you have in mind?" she asks. Her hand is still holding the handle of the restaurant's door.

"You." He doesn't mean to say it aloud; but close to her, experiencing the sweet smells of her, his stomach is rumbling and his body is tightening at the same time. "I mean," he amends, "I want you to come with me. Doesn't matter what we get. How about ice cream? There's a Ben & Jerry's nearby."

It's a decent save, but he swears it was that first thing that slipped out of his mouth, the lascivious one word request, that created the current spark in her eyes.

Job surely in peril, he leads her to a corner table at the Ben & Jerry's ensconced in the labyrinth of tunnels beneath Rockefeller Center and leaves her there while he goes to the restroom to splash cool water on his face. When he returns, she is juggling a book titled *Hung* in one hand and a cone of light brown ice cream in the other.

"What kind is that?" he asks, wondering why she chose to order without waiting for him but secretly grateful. Truthfully, he doesn't like "time-release" desserts like ice cream that melt before he has a chance to savor them properly. They remind him too much of the ephemeral nature of time and maybe the transience of love. This perspective is attributable to his current job and the mental remnants of his undergrad degree in philosophy.

"Café con Leche," she murmurs between licks and reading new sentences, clearly enraptured by both.

"I don't see that on the menu."

"It's not," she says, suddenly taking the uppermost part of the ice cream into her mouth and sucking it into a puckered node of brown. She offers no further explanation for how she came to have a cone of Café con Leche ice cream in an establishment that doesn't appear to serve it, and he decides to enjoy the mystery.

He starts to say something but her mouth distracts him. He doesn't want to get caught watching but she keeps swirling her tongue, as if the flavor tastes especially good right at the tip of it, and he can't help but notice that her mouth seems especially . . . nimble. He makes the mistake of wondering how her mouth would adapt to things other than ice cream and finds himself suddenly thankful to be seated behind a table large enough to give him cover.

She catches him looking, smiles and asks if he wants some. He isn't sure if she is talking about the ice cream or her tongue and senses that her double entendre is very intentional. Before he can respond, she puts the cone to her mouth again, a long lick from the middle of the cone, between her fingers,  to the top of the now-pointy scoop of ice cream, her eyes on his whole time. He feels a flurry of tingles in response—as if someone is rubbing a Popsicle across his skin—and looks away. He reaches for his cell phone simply to buy some recovery time.

There is a text message waiting for him about the cover story on flambé he was supposed to finish copyediting by close of business. He stammers apologies and tells her he has to go back to the office but maybe they can connect again soon. She gazes at him, and then nods to herself, concluding an inner question in the affirmative. Still wordless, she gets up, gathers her things, stands next to him and licks more ice cream from her cone.

"So, let's go," she says.

He doesn't argue with her and doesn't want to, almost hoping there will be someone left in the office to bear witness to his good fortune. By the time they arrive at his building, he thinks better of this idea, and promptly ushers her to a darkened conference room one floor below his office.

Still trying to decide if he should turn the lights on for her comfort or leave them off to help avoid discovery of his indiscretion, he assures her that he won't be long. When she doesn't respond, he turns away from the light switch to find her pressing herself up against the wall-sized windows facing the street. Her dress is thinner than he realized. With the city lights glowing from below and radiating through the dark fabric, he can see the enticing outline of her inner thighs. He glances around for her ice cream cone but doesn't see it, which somehow adds to the dark magic of the moment.

"What are you doing?" he asks her silhouette. His voice is gentle because he doesn't want her to stop.

"I'm always hot," she says. "I like the cool of the glass."

She turns toward him, her body's reduced temperature betrayed by a new set of protrusions, and smiles. "It's like tanning. Now, I'm doing my backside."

Erotically-charged silence swells until he feels like he is being crowded out of the room, no place left to stand but outside in the hallway where the air is thinner and he might be able to breathe more easily. Still, he holds his ground.

"You've been following me all day." Her voice is a husky shadow of what it was before and the bald sexual energy of it makes him want to do inappropriate things. For a moment he is shocked. Her petite frame and innocent countenance offer no immediate corollary for her dramatic shift in vocal intonation.

When the shock wears off and her meaning settles, the heat of embarrassment floods the center of his chest. He is instantly on fire, his armpits prickling with the first, immediate drops of an anxiety-induced sweat. Unsure of how to respond to her observation, he shrugs his shoulders, trying to think of something to say that will not make him sound like the stalker her intoxicating scent has turned him into.

"Slightly eerie," she continues, her octaves dipping even further.

"But extremely flattering." He likes her use of the word "eerie." Not a word usually invoked during casual conversation and even less so during a sensual one. It makes him wonder what else might be uncommon about her. Inside the maze of his mind, all the usual warning bells are going off but there is something about this woman that makes him want to ignore them.

He isn't sure where the confidence comes from to pull her from the window and spin her toward the square conference table behind him as if they are in the middle of a ballroom but she comes to it easily. She stops spinning when the backs of her legs make contact and scoots up onto the table, coming to rest with her legs open and the darkness between her legs, under her skirt, beckoning.

His hunger swells. Again, he is aware of the aroma of her, a heady mix of bread, sugar and liquor. She wriggles in the darkness and before he can make out how it is happening, her dress is pooling into a puddle of silky ripples on the floor beneath her chocolate-colored stilettos.

One step, and he is almost standing between her thighs. He bends to clasp each of her thin ankles in his hands, pulls them up to his waist and uses them to push her away, sliding her along, until she is laying in the center of the glossy, wood-grained table.

The table is small, designed for an intimate meeting of four to six, and her well-toned limbs are long, so she takes up all of it—her pumps bracing at one edge, her knees bending up toward the ceiling and the spiky mini-Mohawk of her hair brushing the opposite edge. Looking down at her, he feels like a man who has been kept starving for days and now finds himself blessed with a bounty of delicacies.

Her brassiere is intricate and lacy with small patches of sheer fabric, one of which simultaneously covers and reveals a silver, bejeweled piercing. The gem at its center glints at him and he realizes that here, finally, is an outer hint to the lascivious spirit he met a few moments ago.

There is only one chair adjacent to the conference table. The others are pushed together behind him in a loose assemblage as if in audience for a presentation . . . or the performance to come. He rolls the chair close to her side and sits down. He wants to examine her curves from this lower angle and savor the view. Leaning forward to smell the now familiar sweetness of her, he is happy to notice that his mouth can reach her easily.

When his lips first touch her shoulder, she moans and he experiences a jolt of pleasure. He has always been partial to moans, the first moan in particular. To him, even more than the first hug or the first kiss, the first moan is a signal and a warning—it is the sound of the heavy door that protects a woman's passion easing itself open at his bidding. And the thrill of unearthing this particular woman's passionate nature runs deep for some reason he doesn't quite understand yet.

He continues down her arm with soft kisses and slow licks. Remarkably, her flavor is even better than her scent—powerful and sugary, and he finds himself fantasizing about eating her as both his meal and his dessert at the beginning and end of every day.

He lifts her arm out of the way and watches her feet writhe as his tongue finds the delicate places along the side of her torso. The further south he travels, the more frenetic the motions of her feet become, her heels making tiny scratches in the burnished wood—a visual punctuation to his every suck and nibble as he rolls his way down the outside of one leg and up the outside of the other leg, one slow inch at a time.

He wishes for condiments: sugar in the raw, licorice, chilled champagne, chocolate-dipped strawberries. These would be for her—tasty surprises he would drop into her mouth when she wasn't expecting it. He doesn't need them, the decadent flavor of her smooth skin is sweet and fulfilling enough to sate him for days.

He travels (and tastes) the circumference of her before rolling his chair back down to where he first pushed her to the middle of the table. He sits there, looking between her upraised legs at her chest and chiseled stomach—both of them rising and falling in time to shallow, affected breaths—until she raises her head to find him. She's been biting her finger and has to stop in order to use her arms as a prop. She needn't have bothered.

Her arms slip out from under her as he tugs her towards him by her ankles. He doesn't stop until her hips are cresting the edge of the table. He looks at her for a long moment before he bends at the waist to do what he has longed to do since he first caught the scent of her body's bouquet.

He licks the smooth fabric of her sheer thong in a slow, lingering way, pretending that her body is the ice cream cone he didn't get at Ben & Jerry's. He keeps licking her through her thong until the moans coming from the table are loud enough to reach the bank of elevators down the hall. Hearing herself, she clutches a fist to her mouth and hesitates just a moment before using her other hand to yank her panties to one side.

Teasing, he takes his time before accepting her bold invitation, but when he comes to it, he does so with enough enthusiasm to make her body twist like a contortionist in a circus, wriggling and bending until her thighs are clutching reflexively against his cheeks so tightly that his jaw aches and burns because of the pressure.

While she is still panting, trying to regroup, trying not to smile, trying not to curse, and his mouth is still singing with the succulent taste of her, he stands and bends over to whisper in her ear.

"Thank you for dessert. Nothing I've ever eaten has tasted as good as you." He isn't sure, but he thinks he sees her blush in response.

Outside, walking arm in arm, giggling every time their eyes meet, he realizes that they haven't spoken since he thanked her, each of them lost in their own molasses-thick morass of decadent thoughts. He lets the rest of it be unspoken too. He leads her all the way to his apartment, closes the bedroom curtains, turns on all the lights and plans to make a meal (and dessert) of her for the rest of his life.

Here, he thinks, is finally a dessert that will last him forever.

Phone, Sex, Chocolate
by Catherine Lundoff

"Really?" I ask, trying not to let my voice squeak. I am pushing tiny chunks of chocolate inside myself, up where you will never go.

Not that I let myself believe that, not really. Your voice purrs in my ear, "Yeah. I mean you got to wonder how some people become managers . . . " Blah, blah, blah about the inanity, the wonder of your day. About the people who have pieces of you that I will never have.

I shift the phone and rock my hips slightly, working the chocolate until I can feel it melt inside me. I imagine your tongue mixing the sticky sweetness in my cunt, tasting and savoring with each swipe, each compact circle. I dip my fingers inside, then bring them to my lips, wanting to taste what you taste, if only you were where I wanted you to be.

I lick my chocolate-flavored juices from my fingertips and smile at the phone. The chocolate is the key. Without it, I'm just another office drone with a bad crush on someone further up the corporate food chain. With it, I'm a goddess, a cocoa-flavored glory who no sane woman would be able to resist. Not even a straight one. I forcibly dismiss your husband's face from my mind. When I'm not on the phone with you, I like the guy, but right now he's a most unwelcome distraction.

You ask me a question and I murmur back something you take for "Yes." It's part of what makes you a star in our world: you only hear "Yes." Even "No" is just on the route to "Yes." I wish I could do that. Maybe then you'd be here licking the melting fondue sweetness oozing out of me instead of being just a sexy voice in my ear.

I brace my feet against the arm of the couch and rub a little harder. I don't want to come, not yet anyway. Not with you on the phone. You might stop calling me if you knew and I don't think I could stand that. But I want to get as close as I can while you're still on the other end of the line, your voice filling in for your hands, the taste of chocolate on your lips.

My pussy aches around my fingers, body straining for release, for fulfillment. For more chocolate. I break off another piece and place it on my tongue, letting it melt down as I murmur assent to your questions which are not questions. I suspect this is what you like about our talks: I am your audience, your reflection. You look at me and see work-related devotion, nothing more. It makes it harder to fantasize about you at, say, lunch. That never gives me the buzz that talking you on the phone does. Fortunately for my job security.

Once we worked together in the same office, drones together, and then I thought you merely hot. Sometimes I would think of you when I got home, my hands working busily between my legs to call forth a humdrum orgasm. I watched as you got promoted, envying you. Especially since you stayed in touch, tried to put in a word for me here and there, or so you said when you called.

I began calling you back, just once a week, nothing that would set off alarms. Mostly I just wanted to hear your voice. At first I tried to hold up my end of the conversation. Then I began to realize it wasn't necessary for either of us. The sound of your voice is enough. Like chocolate, it's deep and rich, just a little slow. It caresses, it fondles each syllable just the way I wish you would if you were touching me. It can be sweet or bitter, filled with innuendo and gossip like nougat or almonds. Your voice, sure and confident, resonates its way inside me each time we talk, playing me like a guitar.

Just the way it's getting to me now, as a matter of fact. My feet strain against the couch, my legs longing to tighten in a movement that can only be released in a tide of chocolate juice. For a moment, I think of inserting a tiny morsel in my asshole, rendering each orifice so sweet that your imagined tongue cannot resist it. I can almost feel that tongue rimming me, then swiping upward to savor the melted chocolate on my clit, in my aching pussy. My breath comes faster, in little gasps, and I tilt the phone cautiously with my free hand so you don't hear anything.

I wonder if I can come quietly enough that you won't notice that either but that's not how I want to do it. I want to soak the towel under me and spray chocolate all over in a glorious sugary mess, filling my mouth with so much chocolate that my moans are muffled. I want to come like I never do for any of my real lovers, the girlfriends who come and go like shadows in the time between your phone calls. Somehow they never live up to my fantasies.

Tonight, I'm trying something different. I reach for the white chocolate that rests in its foil package next to the dark brown that I usually favor and break off a chunk. It occurs to me to ask you a question. "Do you like chocolate? I mean, like really crave it? When you open the package, do you break off a little piece and roll it around in your mouth before you swallow it? I love that first taste." I subside into your noncommittal response. I mean, who doesn't like chocolate, unless they're allergic or something?

But then I read something else into your answer. Chocolate is a metaphor for me and you can take or leave either of us. I try to imagine a world without the lovely taste of chocolate-covered hazelnuts, orange peels, coffee beans, and for a moment I feel sorry for you. You're missing out on so much, my chocolate-filled pussy just one small part of the greater universe that you will never know.

The white chocolate tidbit joins the dark brown already inside me. Tonight my juices will be a marbled swirl of sticky sweetness and I smile as I picture it. I like to think that you would savor this chocolate more than any old bar out of the foil wrapping. The interplay of its sugary cocoa flavor and my own slightly sour tang would complement each other in a sauce any lover could delight in. My clit groans for fulfillment, buzzing in its nest of sauce until I'm not sure I can hold back much longer.

We make plans for lunch next week and you sign off with some flippant comment about beauty sleep. I drop the phone, sending both hands between my legs to rub soft chocolate on my clit in tight, firm circles. I imagine you in your power suit, taking me on your desk with expensive chocolate dripping onto your memos and I come hard, my back arching against the couch.

Sometimes when I get off the phone, I dare to imagine touching you, trailing chocolate sauce up your thighs and down between your legs. Perhaps even drizzling it on your nipples. I lick until I am surfeited, until I can't stand the taste of chocolate any more, then I keep licking anyway because it's what you want. The smell of chocolate is overwhelming, filling my nose and throat until I can't smell it without thinking of you.

I grab another piece and slip it under my tongue, sending my hand between my legs again. Now my fingers are sticky, frantic, and my clit burns hot and sugary sweet in its nest of fudge-swirled flesh. Little shocks fly up and down my thighs as I stiffen, then relax, then stiffen them again, rigid until the moment of release.

This time, I bellow through the chocolate, howl my longings at the walls of my apartment. My back arches and I convulse against the towels under me, rubbing chocolate juice all over my bare ass and thighs. The piece beneath my tongue melts its way down my throat and for a moment, I know this is how you would taste. I come again, laughing between gasps.

When I can't stand any more, when my sugar-flavored flesh twitches away from the touch of my own fingers and your imagined caresses, I head for the shower, dropping the towels into the hamper alongside their companions: two towels per phone call. When I am done scouring the chocolate from my body, done scrubbing my obsession with your voice from my ears, I dry myself off and go back to the living room. I place two clean towels on the coffee table and put the chocolate back in the tins where I store it. I force myself not to listen for the phone to ring.

Old-Fashioned Fudge
by Tsaurah Litzky

We were lying side by side and she was holding me. Once in a while, she squeezed, gently, drawing her fingers more closely around my prick as it softened in her little hand.

"I don't want to let it go," she said. "I'm memorizing your particular shape, so I can carry the memory of your cock with me wherever I go."

I was so happy. Every time I was with her, I felt like I was Superman and she was Lois and it was our wedding night. "I know what," I said, "I'll have a model made for you the way those guys did of their equipment in the 60's, what did they call those guys, plaster casters? You can put my plaster cast in your purse and carry it everywhere. It can be your lucky charm."

She cut in, "But you're always giving me gifts, wonderful gifts, like the old-fashioned razor you got just for shaving me, and the strap-on you already let me use on you three times. I've hardly given you anything. Remember, it's your birthday next Wednesday and it's the first time we're spending a birthday together. I want to give you something special."

She was right; it was the first birthday we were spending together. When we met I thought a nerdy writer like me could never keep a femme fatale like her interested for a week. Yet now, here we are six months later, and she has her toothbrush in my medicine cabinet and doesn't want to let go of my cock.

"What can I get you," she went on, "what in the whole wide world? What do you want the most?" I didn't tell her she was what I wanted the most, she was the air I wanted to breathe.

"I don't know. A new iPod or some Ray-Bans?"

"No, she answered, "I want to give you something hot, something sexy. I know just the thing." In her excitement, she clenched her hand, squeezing my sex so hard I winced.

"Sorry," she said, and bent her lovely head and kissed the tip and then she went on. "I know the perfect gift. I know you like Charlene." Charlene was her best friend. "And she thinks you are just adorable. I'll invite her to play with

us. She adores orgies, 'multiples' is what she likes to call them. Isn't that a great idea? Wouldn't that be your best birthday gift ever?"

The thought of satisfying my powerful little Queen of Sheba and her five-foot-eleven, thirty-eight triple-D friend who runs triathalons was terrifying. "Absolutely not," I hastened to object. "Never, I don't like orgies, they are er, er . . . too impersonal. I want whatever you give me to involve just the two of us."

"Well, then, what do you want?" she asked.

"I'm thinking," I told her, "I just put my thinking cap on."

Suddenly, I knew what I wanted. I love chocolate almost as much as I love the sweet candy between her legs. My very favorite chocolate delight is fudge, good old-fashioned fudge. My mother always made it for holidays and for my birthday. She used bitter-sweet chocolate and plenty of walnuts. Before I even tasted any snatch, I always thought it would taste like that good old-fashioned fudge, cocoa sweet and grainy with a hint of fresh nutty flavor. In the 12th grade, when I finally got a real taste of pussy, when I went with Lila from the projects to the field behind the 7-11, she tasted like stale peanuts. I was so disappointed. Luckily, I discovered as I went along, that snatch can also have a delicious taste.

"Fudge," I told my Queen of Sheba. "I want you to make me some delicious fudge, dark chocolate fudge with walnuts, like my mother used to make."

"But baby," she said, "You know I can't cook. I don't really know how. I was raised on take-out. I can make hard-boiled eggs and tuna salad, that's it."

"Well then, that's perfect," I said, "for you who don't know how to cook to make a special effort and cook some fudge just for me on my birthday, that's a wonderful gift."

"How?" she interjected. "I won't have time for cooking school."

I reassured her, "You don't have to go to cooking school, just get a good recipe. I'll help you."

"I don't know," she said, "it doesn't sound very sexy."

"It will be," I answered, the idea taking shape in my mind. "You're going to make the fudge wearing nothing but a frilly little white apron and, oh yeah, those real high leopard skin stilettos of yours. I'll sit at the kitchen table drinking scotch and watch."

Now she smiled at me, she downright grinned. "I get it," she said. "Maybe you won't wear any clothes either and when the fudge is done we'll eat it together."

"That's right," I said.

"Maybe you'll put a piece in my candy jar and eat it out of there," she suggested. I felt my cock begin to stiffen once more; she still had it in her hand. She felt it too, and squeezed. "What have we here?" she asked, already knowing the answer. "Ready for an encore?"

"Is fudge sweet?" I answered.

She sat up and got a condom out of the drawer in my bedside table. She tore it open and then put it between her lips. I watched her slide it on me with her mouth, her tongue pushing the latex further down. Just feeling her hot mouth on me made me jump and twist.

"No," she said, "not yet." She got up on her hands and knees beside me, arched her back, making her tight, sleek butt poke up in the air.

"Now," she said, "Let's do it like the doggies do." Her breasts hung down like teats, and I put a hand out and grabbed one. I pulled hard; she likes it when I hurt her a little.

"Okay, bitch," I said. I got up on my knees and knelt between her legs. "Good bitch," I said, and then I pulled her ass cheeks open and held them apart so I could watch that dark little hole at the same time as I watched my cock move in and out of the larger hole below. It looked so nasty, so nice and nasty. In an instant, I was so ready to poke her. I held her hips firmly for balance.

"Woof, woof," I barked. "I'm Lassie," I said. "I'm Rin-Tin-Tin. I'm Cujo," and then I slid it in.

After, she nested against me. I was on my back and she was curled under my arm.

"I really have no idea how to make that fudge for your birthday," she said. "You better help me find a recipe. I don't even know where to look."

"That's no problem," I told her. "I have a great cookbook." I went into the living room and got my mother's worn old 1946 *Joy of Cooking*. I brought it into the bedroom and put the book in bed beside her. I turned to the candy section and quickly located the fudge recipes.

"There are so many of them," she said. "Here, how about this one called Divinity Fudge? What a great name. Oh, I have to use a double boiler. What's a double boiler?"

I read down the page. "We'll find an easier one," I told her. "Here's a recipe called Old-Fashioned Fudge, just what I like, and all we need to cook it in is a large heavy pan and I have one of those." Her eyes followed my finger down the page.

"Old-Fashioned Fudge," she read aloud. "Sugar, salt, chocolate, milk, vanilla extract. I can get all those. What I have to do next sounds pretty easy; put the ingredients in a big mixing bowl, mix them all up and put the pan on the stove. After that, I cover the pan and cook covered for two to three minutes, then I take the cover off, lower the heat and cook until the fudge gets to a soft ball stage."

She pressed her hot little rack closer to me. "But how do we know when the fudge gets to the soft ball stage?" It was true; she didn't know how to cook.

"It says so right here," I read to her. "There is a fine overall bubbling pattern, and then we take it off the heat." She finished reading the sentence for me. "When it's cool, add four tablespoons butter, beat it all up, and add a teaspoon of vanilla and the walnuts. Pour into a buttered pan and cut it before it cools."

Her brow furrowed, "I don't know," she said. "There seems like a lot of steps. Why don't we just invite Charlene over? I bet she knows how to make fudge."

"No, no way," I said, a little too sharply. "All we need to do is follow the instructions in the book, that's the big secret to being a good cook. I'll help you," I told her. "It's not hard." She put her hand on my belly and moved it down into the hairy jungle below.

"Hah, wrong, wrong, wrong, and three times in a row. Go Cujo, go," she said as she straddled me.

In the few days before my birthday, she phoned several times. Should she get sweet butter or salted butter, she wanted to know. Should she get walnuts in the shell or the already shelled kind? I answered her questions and asked her if she wanted me to buy her the frilly white apron.

"Not necessary," she answered. "I already have a nice one, silk organza trimmed with French lace."

I felt that little vein in my neck begin to pulse, the one that meant I was getting angry. I wanted to ask her who got her that apron? Who else did you wear it for? I knew it was better if I didn't know. With a supreme effort. I managed to stop myself.

Instead, I said, "I'm going to treat myself to a birthday bottle of Glenfiddich. I know you like it, too."

"I won't let you buy it, no way," she shot back. "It's your birthday and after we eat the fudge you can pour the Glenfiddich all over me and lick it off."

"I love your imagination even more than your wonderful tits," I told her.

On my birthday, I cleaned my apartment, then I dressed for my special date.

I put on my favorite navy blue sweatpants and the muscle t-shirt she gave me that said *Sex Machine*. She rang my doorbell at eight o'clock. I already had the big mixing bowl, the measuring spoons and the measuring cup on the kitchen counter. I had placed *The Joy of Cooking* next to it, open to the page with the fudge recipe. The pan was waiting on the stove.

Her arms were filled with packages. "Let me take those from you," I said.

"Okay," she answered, "but then I have to give you a birthday kiss."

I took the packages from her and she followed me into the kitchen. As soon as I put the lot of them on the kitchen counter, she was on me, standing on her tiptoes to find my mouth.

She opened my lips with her wily tongue and fucked my mouth with it until I was breathless with wanting her. By the time she pulled her mouth off mine, the rod between my legs was big as an eggbeater. I found my voice again. "I have a better idea," I said. "Why don't I unpack this stuff while you change into that frilly white apron?"

"Whatever you say, birthday boy," she answered. She patted my package affectionately and left the room.

Soon there was a quart of milk, a stick of butter, the sugar, the salt, a package of Baker's semisweet chocolate and a tin of shelled walnuts on the counter. Then there was the bottle of Glenfiddich, I had just finished pouring out a nice shot for each of us when she came back into the room.

The apron she had tied around her waist was transparent. I could see the plump V between her legs covered with that silky dark hair. I could see her navel, a tiny perfect star just below the waistband of the apron. Her pendulous bare breasts floated above, her perfect nipples two cocoa bonbons I wanted to suck. I handed her glass to her and picked up mine. "To Good Old-Fashioned Fudge," I toasted. We drank.

"And now, I better get to work," she said. She bent over the cookbook for a few minutes, studying it. Her elegant brow furrowed in concentration. Carefully, she poured the right amount of sugar into the measuring cup. She seemed afraid to pick it up, as if it would explode.

"How am I doing?" she asked while she slowly poured salt into a tablespoon.

"Just great," I told her. Finally she got all the ingredients in the bowl. Biting her luscious lower lip, she seized the wooden spoon and with great determination plunged it into the chocolate mass. She started to churn. "Nothing is mixing," she sighed.

"Keep at it," I told her, but first finish your Scotch." She followed my suggestion and soon she had that wooden spoon whirling. She added the vanilla, stirred some more. "How's that?" she asked. It smelled like fudge heaven.

"Perfect," I told her. "Now pour it into the pan, use the spoon to get it off the side of the bowl." Her titties hung low over the pan, swaying slightly. I wanted to throw her to the floor and stick my big spoon between her breasts, but before I could, she put the cover on the pan and asked me a question.

"How do you light the stove?" she said. "Mine is electric."

"This is how," I answered her as I turned on the burner.

"You make everything so simple," she said. She started to put the bowl and baking things in the sink.

"Wait," I said. "We get to lick the bowl and the spoon first. It's nearly as good as eating the fudge." I put the spoon in the bowl, handed it to her and pushed her ahead of me into the living room. I sat her down on the couch and sat down right next to her. I put a hand around her shoulder and with the other hand, I raised the spoon to her mouth.

"Now lick this," I said. I watched her pretty pink tongue spear some of the stuff and carry it back between her lips.

"Scrumptious," she said. "And it's not even cooked. Now you try it." She scraped some onto the spoon and handed it to me.

"Even better then my mother used to make," I said.

"Flattery will get you everywhere," she replied. "Now that we've got the spoon clean, there's still some left in the bowl. Why don't you smear it on me, and then lick me off."

"I don't want to soil your pretty apron," I said. "I better take it off." I reached behind her, untied the bow, whisked the apron off and there it was, her altar of love, my garden of delight.

"Open your legs," I said, and she obeyed. Her labia were already glistening with her sweet juices. Using my fingers, I cleaned what fudge mixture was left from inside the bowl and rubbed it over her labia. I covered the inside of her clit and the inside of her cunt with the stuff. Gently, I rubbed it on, I rubbed and rubbed. She sighed with pleasure. Then she reached out a hand and cupping my balls in her palm, she teased her nimble fingers up my prick.

I bent my mouth right down into her; I licked and nibbled, I gobbled and savored. She opened wider, thrusting up to meet my tongue. Her fingers closed around me and she started moving them up and down, down and up. There was still some fudge left on her clit but before I could get to it, she started groaning low in her throat, making that purring sound that meant she was coming and I couldn't stop myself from joining her, shooting my cream across her tummy. After a few minutes she said, "Rub it in, rub it in."

I was doing just that, rubbing her tits, enjoying the view of her sprawled out like the Naked Maja on my ratty blue couch, when we were disturbed by a loud ringing sound coming from the kitchen.

"What's that?" she asked, startled. "An alarm clock?"

"No," I said, comprehension dawning. "It's my freakin' smoke alarm."

We ran into the kitchen. It was all smoky. Quickly, I opened the window, then I dashed to the stove and turned off the flame. I took the pan off the burner. The fudge was a charred black mess.

"Oh no," she said. She looked so downcast. "There goes your fudge. I wanted it to be perfect." I hastened to reassure her.

"Don't feel bad," I said. "We can always make more fudge. This is already my best birthday yet." I took her hand in mine and led her to my bedroom.

Mulled Wine
by Dominic Santi

"Why does your dick taste like mulled wine?"

If Glen and I were monogamous, that would be a problem. Fortunately, we're not. So I grinned when I looked down at him and said, "I stopped at Jake and Karl's Christmas party on the way home."

"Oh, indeed!" Glen leaned forward, once more sucking my dick into his mouth. His short blond curls bobbed against his Santa hat and his blue eyes twinkled up at me. I loved watching his cheek bulge out as my dick hardened on his hot, wet tongue. He sucked me long and slowly, like he was drawing the flavor off my skin to differentiate each of the specific tastes.

"Cinnamon, clove," he laughed, pulling back so his saliva dripped off my dickhead. "Perhaps a hint of allspice."

I shivered as he flicked his tongue down my shaft, like a snake smelling. He paused to suck my skin into his mouth, massaging with his tongue before he worked his way back up, and swallowed me deep. He was panting when he finally came up for air.

"How's about you give me all the gory details, hot stuff, while I feast on your exceptionally delicious dick and get you naked." He once more kissed down my shaft, this time untying my shoes with one hand. "I'm in the mood for something festive."

I saw no reason to argue with the man sucking my dick. Just as I'd expected, Glen had ambushed me when I walked in the door. "Festive" barely began to describe his attire. He was naked except for the Santa hat and a shiny steel ring encircling the base of his cock and balls. A large pair of jingle bells hung from the bottom of the ring, swinging merrily on red and green curly ribbon below his freshly shaved scrotum and his upthrust cock. On one nut he'd painted "LUV," on the other, "U," in what I had no doubt was the spearmint-flavored glow-in-the-dark red body paint I'd seen him admiring when he was perusing the latest and greatest at his favorite online sex toy store last week.

"God, I love the way you have fun," I laughed. The sound segued into a moan as he deep throated me again. He hummed the first bars of "Jingle Bells" along with the CD he had playing in the background, his voice vibrating over me until I was shaking. Then he pulled off my dripping dick and slid the first shoe over my foot.

"The wine, my love . . ."

I balanced my hands on his hat as he deftly peeled off my shoes and socks and disposed of the pants puddled at my ankles.

"Jack sent me an e-mail I couldn't refuse as we were closing up for the day. I followed him home, reminding him you and I had plans, so I couldn't stay late." I looked down meaningfully into Glen's sparkling baby blues. He slurped my dick back into his mouth, rewarding me with a sucking kiss that left me shaking. "B-by the time we got there, Karl and his buddies had a fucking orgy going on. There must have been 30 people roaming around the house, and it was barely six." I threw off my jacket and tie as Glen sat up and yanked open the buttons on my shirt. I tossed that aside as well. "Four guys in elf hats were straddling the coffee table, trying to fuck in a daisy chain to 'Santa Claus is Coming to Town.' Fantastic hors d'oeuvres, bowls of mint-flavored condoms—and lots of mulled wine. Fuck, that feels so good!"

I moaned, grabbing Glen's head as he again dove down on my dick. He was laughing so hard I was surprised he didn't choke. I fucked in and out of his mouth, panting hard. "I told Jack I was only going to play for a while, and I didn't want to come as that would interfere with our plans here. That's when he dunked my dick in his wine and told me they'd be going strong all night, if we wanted to 'come' by later." As Glen looked quizzically up at me, I locked my fingers in his hair. "Up to you, sweetie. At the moment, I'm right where I want to be." I tipped his chin up so our eyes met and held. "I wouldn't miss our holiday tradition for the world."

Nodding, he winked and went back to licking my dick. Then he licked his way up my belly, up my chest and neck until we were swallowing each other like anacondas. Still kissing me, he grabbed hold of my dick and led me into the living room.

A fire was blazing in the fireplace. The coffee table had been pushed aside. In its place was Glen's exercise mat covered with red satin sheets. A pile of holiday throw pillows on the mat glowed in the firelight. On the floor on a short wooden tray were two full crystal water goblets and a silver bowl of unwrapped candy canes. Still holding my dick, Glen led me onto the middle of the mat and pushed me down on my back. Facing me, he dropped to his knees and straddled my head, so his scrotum hovered over my mouth.

"Read your Christmas cards, hot stuff," he said, lowering himself until his painted balls were almost touching my lips and those damn jingle balls rolled forward to tickle my nose.

I could read, all right. "I love you, too," I laughed, sticking out my tongue. As my taste buds exploded with the taste of mint, Glen squatted further down. I filled my mouth with the firm, smooth heat of his low-hanging balls. He moaned as I washed them clean, licking and sucking with the same fervor he'd shown my shaft, tangling my tongue on those damn bells and ribbons, and worrying my lips over the body-warmed metal of his cock ring. Even over the mint, I could smell sweat and soap and the scent that was so uniquely my man's.

When Glen shoved a pillow under my head, I groaned in anticipation. "I'm going to choke on these fucking bells."

"No, you won't," he laughed. He grabbed a pillow for himself and turned around. The bells jingled merrily as he again positioned himself over my chest. He squatted back, his cheeks spread wide, revealing the beautiful pink pucker aiming right for my mouth. His warm hard cock pressed against me and those damn bells rolled back beneath my chin. I resisted the urge to lick as he leaned forward and lifted my legs, spreading them wide and bending them back under his arms. He's just enough shorter than me that we fit together perfectly. My hard-on pressed against his chest.

"Merry Christmas, love," he whispered, blowing gently. I arched up, shivering as his lips came down. Then he was kissing my hole. With a heartfelt moan, I stuck out my tongue and indulged in the long, slow lick I'd been longing for.

I felt Glen's groan in every bone in my body. His hole was beautiful, a tight little pucker. It swelled up warm and tangy and sensitive when I worried it with my tongue. As I wet him to glistening with my spit, Glen's kisses deepened. I pulled my legs further back, opening myself wider to him as he dug in deep.

"Fuck, that feels good." I gasped as he drilled his tongue into me. Putting my fingers on either side of his spit-covered pucker, I spread his cheeks wide apart. He was tonguing me harder, wiggling his ass, leaning back further as I stretched him. I licked one finger, put it in the center of his pucker, and rubbed.

Glen went wild. He rocked his chest over my hard-on, leaning back as he feverishly licked my hole.

"So good!" he panted, squirming uncontrollably as I pressed my fingertip in. As much as Glen loved sixty-nining, his concentration went all to hell when I penetrated him. He licked and sucked my hole for all he was worth, but every other thought process in his brain drained south to where my lips and fingers were. I slowly spread his sphincters, working in both index fingers up to the first knuckle as I gradually stretched him open and lapped my way into him. What he was doing to my ass was driving me nuts. Glen went wild, moaning and writhing and tongue fucking me as the muffled bells jingled against my neck. I washed him with spit until his hole was dripping and I was shaking. Then I reached into the silver bowl.

The candy canes had been Glen's idea. He'd spent hours on the Internet, researching and later taste and "environmental" testing various brands until he found the perfect ones that were wide and strong and smooth enough for what he had in mind. The week before our first Christmas together, he'd seduced me into another of the mutual rim jobs we loved so much. And he'd brought out his *piece de resistance*. I'd never come so hard in my life.

He moved in with me the next day. Every year since, we'd celebrated our anniversary the same way. I knew what was coming tonight. So did Glen. He groaned at the soft clink as I wet the candy cane in the water glass. I kept licking, gentling his hole open even as I spread his cheeks wide with the fingers of one hand. Then I pushed his hips slightly up, ignoring those damn bells as I touched the wet candy to his pucker. Very slowly, I twirled the tip of the cane.

"Oh, FUCK!"

His pucker clenched, quivering as I rubbed the sticky peppermint into the spit. I licked around the stick, careful not to penetrate him, my mouth tingling with the onslaught of mint. Glen panted and shook above me. When my lips were as sticky as his hole, I licked him wet again. Then I blew softly over his skin.

Glen jerked up hard, crying out as I turned the cane sideways and rubbed it back and forth. Each time I blew, he shuddered.

"You know what's coming next, hon," I whispered. I dunked the candy cane in the water again. Spreading wide, I again dug my tongue in deep. He was so warm inside, so smooth on my tongue as I drilled through his trembling gate. I sucked the sides of his sphincter, savoring the flavor of his skin blending with the mint on my taste buds. This time, when I withdrew my tongue, I had the dripping candy cane waiting. I touched it to his now loose and slippery hole, and slowly, deliberately twirled it in.

Glen bucked up, yelling and clenching his ass muscles as I gradually worked a good inch of the candy cane past his now darkly flushed and slightly swollen pucker. I took the candy out, tonguing his minty, hot hole while I dunked the cane in the water again. Then I fucked the slippery, sticky toy back into him, slowly working my way up. As his tongue flicked erratically over me, I slowly and relentlessly slid the peppermint inside him, watching the red and white stripes disappear to the two-inch "safety" line Glen had painstakingly marked on the cane.

"You like?" I growled, keeping up the long, slow fucks as I licked my minty spit up the back of his balls and over the metal ring surrounding the base of his rock-hard dick.

"Oh, god, yes!" he groaned, grinding his cock against me as I twirled the cane in and out of his ass like a barber pole. "It's hot, and it's cold, and it burns, and I love it! Fuck, I love it!"

With his whole body shaking, he jerked my legs further up and drove his tongue into me. I've been a slut as many years as my sweetie has. At the feel of his tongue, I relaxed my hole and let him take me to heaven. His hand fumbled as he reached for his crystal glass. He swore loudly as he knocked it over. Bracing himself on one elbow, he dunked a candy cane into my water glass. Then he was between my legs again, his elbows pressing my thighs back and open as his fingers spread my asslips. I could feel the hint of heat on his fingers where he gently caressed my sphincter. In front of me, his asshole still fluttered ecstatically over the candy cane buried two full inches up his butt.

"Don't move the cane," he choked out, licking my hole as he wet me. "I need to concentrate."

Holding the handle of the candy, I left the cane buried in his ass and stilled my hand. I kissed the sticky, mint-flavored flesh in back of his balls as I braced myself for what I knew was coming. But even with all the times we'd done this, I could never really be prepared. I felt the delicious twirl and slide at the same time I felt the heat. Then I felt the cold and the burn and the vibration of Glen's laughter. I yelled and bucked up and the cane slid in its full two inches in one long glide.

I thought I'd never stop shaking. Glen fucked me until I was twitching so much I could hardly breathe. As my balls climbed my shaft, he shifted, just enough for me to suck his cock into my mouth. I tasted mint as his dick slid down my throat. I felt the burning cold, wet heat of his mouth closing over my shaft. Then we were a frenzy of fucking, sucking, juicy holes and dicks as we ground together and sucked each other off and fucked each other with those fucking candy canes until we sent each other into orbit with orgasms that literally had me seeing stars. My balls drained themselves dry and I sucked his come down my throat until he collapsed on top of me. We lay there for the longest time, totally blissed out and holding each other tight, covered in sticky minty come with the candy canes still buried up our butts. Finally Glen lifted his head.

"That is really starting to burn," he laughed. He was still out of breath as he clenched and unclenched against the candy cane. I dutifully slid the cane free, then tenderly licked his swollen asshole clean. My mouth tingled as much as my hole did where Glen was now washing me the same way.

He pressed his ass back against my face as he once more kissed my throbbing hole. As our pulses slowed, he turned and snuggled into my arms. His hat had fallen off somewhere during the festivities. When he worked the cock ring off, I threw it and those damn jingle bells across the room. We lay there for a long time, watching the fire and kissing, and laughing when we squirmed at the stimulation in our assholes. It felt good holding him, even though I wasn't tired.

Actually, I wasn't tired at all. And when we kissed, I tasted a hint of mulled wine spices from my cock on his lips, along with the peppermint.

"You know," I said, rubbing my fingers in the sticky come and candy juice on his belly. "It's not really that late."

His laugh told me he'd been thinking the same thing. "I'll bank the fire. But no fucking at the party. I have no idea how the peppermint affects rubbers." At my raised eyebrows, he shrugged and grinned. "No matter who you have sex with tonight, I want you feeling my love juice burning your ass. Just like I feel yours." He gave me a quick kiss, then bent to pick up his goblet.

"Merry Christmas, sweetie. Let's go find us a holiday orgy."

Sugar on Snow
by Sacchi Green

Powdery snowflakes swirled thick and fast, clinging to our jackets, clustering on woolly hats and even Lea's long eyelashes like a storm of confectioners' sugar. "You're in for it now!" I called back to her. "It's too late to get away, even if your car would start."

I slowed my pace to let her come up beside me, skis swishing rhythmically along the cross-country trail. "You saw me pocket that distributor rotor, didn't you, Kit?" Her face, or what I could see of it through the snowflakes, glowed pink with cold air and exertion. The glint of mischief in her hazel eyes seemed to melt away the twenty-five years since we'd been college roommates; it seemed impossible that the smooth hair concealed by the bright knit hat was silver now, and short, instead of the long fall of pale gold I remembered so well.

"Oh yeah, I didn't miss that little maneuver," I said. "And then I checked your car while everybody else was indoors packing and trying to persuade you to accept a lift. If you wanted to stay here with me badly enough to fake an excuse, why should I blow the whistle on you?"

The other two old friends from college had left the mini-reunion at my place two days ahead of schedule, when the morning news had upgraded the weather forecast from light snow to a potential blizzard. They had families and work to consider. My own new assignment with the National Forest Service was right here, in the New England of my birth, after years of moving from region to region. The few relationships I'd managed had been deliberately temporary. Lea was taking a long break from burnout as head nurse in a big city hospital, and her second marriage had dissolved several years ago. Neither of us needed to be anyplace else any time soon.

We coasted down the incline to my cabin beside the ice-edged river. Her car and my pick-up truck were already coated with a thick layer of white as frothy as meringue on a lemon pie.

"I was pretty sure you knew," Lea said, coming to a stop and releasing the bindings on her skis. "Maybe I even wanted you to know. And since you didn't say anything right away, I hoped it meant you didn't mind. Thanks for keeping it to yourself. I acted on impulse and then felt silly for not just saying right out that I wanted to stay."

"You *were* silly. What could make more sense than riding out the storm here, where electricity is only one option? We have enough firewood and food to last until plowed roads or spring, whichever comes first." I managed to maintain a light tone, no matter how fiercely I needed to know what Lea was up to. Once upon a time we'd been close enough to nearly read each other's minds, but that was very long ago. When she had finally understood how much beyond youthful experimentation I wanted of her, and I had realized how much I couldn't have, our friendship had survived, but on a carefully superficial level. Over the last decade our communications had dwindled into annual notes on Christmas cards.

"What's sense got to do with it?" Lea flashed a grin, but it faded quickly. "It's not just a matter of shelter from the storm, either. Or . . . well, in a way, maybe it is, but . . ."

She paused so long that I picked up my skis and started up the steps. Lea followed into the screened porch. "Well, I'm glad you're here," I said, keeping a firm lid on the hopes and speculations roiling inside. Lea had been under a lot of stress; I wasn't sure she knew herself what she wanted. "We can do some catching up."

She shook her head. Soft snow slumped from her hat across her face, like frosting sliding down a cake still hot from the oven. I reached reflexively to wipe it away, barely stifling the urge to lick it from her cheeks, just as she raised her own hand. When I started to pull back, her fingers wrapped around my thumb and held tight. "Not catching up," she said. "Starting over." She let go and gestured toward the white expanse outside. "Doesn't the snow make you think of new beginnings, pristine, untrodden paths, unmarked pages?"

A gust of wind hit us with needles of that pristine snow blowing right through the screens. The flakes were smaller now, sharper, and coming down even harder.

"It makes me think of stoking the fire," I said, shaking the snow from my hat and jacket and opening the door. "And getting in where it's warm. C'mon." She was going to have to be more explicit than that before I could lower my guard against disappointment. But once inside, kneeling to fit logs carefully into the woodstove in the living room, I looked over my shoulder long enough to say, "Lea, you know you made your mark on my pages long ago. Indelibly."

"I do know it, Kit." She was already mixing leftovers from last night's communal feast into some sort of stew. "You don't know how many times I've wondered, over the last few years . . . wanted to reach out . . . But we seemed to have traveled so far apart."

She stood beside me, stirring the pot on the woodstove, apparently getting into the spirit of rustic living even before it was necessary. The past three days she'd been cooking and eating with such enthusiasm that one friend had teased that her taste buds must have just recently recovered from the long-ago trauma of college meals, since she seemed to be making up for lost time. It did seem to be an irony of nature that Lea, so fixated on food, was still as elegantly lithe as a cougar, while I, who could hike all day on a handful or two of trail mix, bore more resemblance to a silver-tipped grizzly.

I stood up stiffly, brushing wood chips from my hands onto my pants legs. The hell with playing it cool when the heat building inside me mirrored the flames licking at the wood in the stove. "We don't seem to be all that far apart now," I said, just beginning to reach for Lea when she turned right into the circle of my arms. My cheek brushed her smooth hair as she burrowed her face into my shoulder, and for a moment I thought she might be crying, but when she raised her head her lips were curved into a little smile so delectable that I had to taste it; and then, a mere taste wasn't enough.

The kiss was so sweetly searing that we couldn't bear to break it even when the lights went out. Power lines somewhere had gone down under the snow-laden weight of falling branches, but the glow through the glass front of the stove was enough for us. The sound and smell of boiling stew beginning to splatter over and scorch, though, did the trick. We pulled apart, and I grabbed a holder and moved the pot to the brick hearth.

"I suppose we should eat some," Lea said, breathlessly. "To keep our strength up."

"We could definitely need it," I agreed, lighting a couple of candles from the chimney mantle to place on the folding table pulled close to the stove. Then, while Lea ladled stew into bowls and sliced some bread, I opened out the futon couch I'd been sleeping on for a few days, leaving the bedrooms to my guests. Tonight I was hoping I wouldn't even need the excuse of staying close to the fire's warmth to keep from sleeping there alone.

"This is so great," Lea said after about half her meal had been devoured. I'd just dunked my bread a few times and nibbled at it. "It's so. . . so . . . " she waved her spoon as though it might scoop the words she wanted from the air.

"Cozy?" I suggested. "Romantic?"

"Yes, those, but . . . so *right*, too," she said. "I can't tell you how grateful I am to the storm for chasing the others away."

I shoved back my chair and gave up any pretense of eating. "I only invited them to get you to come. So you wouldn't worry."

"Worry about what?" Candlelight flickered across her smile and danced in her eyes. She knew perfectly well what I meant.

"About this." I stood, lifted the whole table aside, and pulled her up from her chair. She raised her face for a kiss, but I resisted, unbuttoning her shirt and spreading it open. "And this." I pressed my lips into the hollow of her throat, savoring its tenderness, getting hungrier and hungrier for more. She shrugged the shirt right off while my hands pushed her sports bra up out of the way so I could cup her small breasts.

"Wait a minute . . ." Lea pulled the bra off over her head, and while her arms were raised I caught one firm nipple after the other in my mouth. She gasped, then tried to keep me from drawing away, gripping my short hair to force me closer, but I pulled her hands free and stretched them far apart.

"I need to look at you. It's been so long . . ."

"And I'm so much older now," she said wryly, but didn't flinch from my gaze. There was no need. The set of her head, the curve of cheek and throat and shoulder and peaked breast, had been my standard of desire ever since they'd been imprinted on my memory. If I noticed any changes—the very slightest filling out and softening, perhaps, of her breasts?—they just enhanced her appeal.

"And so much more enticing, too," I said, letting her arms drop so that I could stroke her from shoulder blades downward until my hands slid inside the waistband of her jeans and pressed into the curves of her buttocks. "In the firelight your skin has such a delicious glow, like an apricot glaze."

I eased back just a little and bent again to taste her breasts.

"Yes, a definite flavor of apricots, but nectarine-sized apricots, sweet and complex." I sucked gently on an eager nipple.

"Ah . . . Kit . . . you're making me so hungry! But what I want are soft, ripe mangoes." Lea's quick fingers tugged my shirttail from my pants and got right underneath to my skin, working upward until she had a firm grip on my breasts. Each lick and suck I gave her was echoed by sharp tweaks that sent tongues of flame streaking through my body. Too soon, sensation overrode both concentration and balance, and we toppled onto the futon in a tangle of limbs and a frantic shedding of clothing.

The wind outside howled down from the mountains through the river valley, making huge branches thrash and rattling the damper in the chimney, but we scarcely noticed. With my cheek pressed against Lea's breast, I could feel the pounding of her heart

and hear the ragged sounds forming in her chest even before they left her throat. I moved my hand insistently, stroking, squeezing, then probing into her slick, hot depths, keeping time at first with the arching and thrashing of her hips and then increasing my tempo and demand until, with a cascade of rough cries, she clenched her cunt around my fingers in a spasm hard enough to trap them.

I held her close against me until her breathing finally slowed. Even the wind had dwindled almost to silence, and the whisper of falling snow against the windows was as gentle as the stroke of my fingers through her hair.

Lea's soft voice drew me upward through layers of sleep.

"I've been watching you dream," she said. The fire had burned down to bright cherry coals, its light bronzing the silver helmet of her hair.

"Am I dreaming now?" I murmured, still drifting.

She lay propped on one elbow, blankets sliding down her shoulder. The scent of her warm body flooded my senses with memory. Better than dreaming. I reached out to pull her close, but the goose bumps on her arm reminded me of what the fire's sunset glow meant. I pulled the blankets higher over her shoulders and slipped out from under them myself.

"Time for more wood," I said unnecessarily.

"I was about to do it," she said. "I didn't want to wake you. I'm not quite sure of the etiquette of fiddling with someone else's fire."

"Don't worry. Anything goes in a blizzard." My flesh tingled under her interested gaze as I stooped to the woodpile and knelt before the glass-fronted stove.

When the flames leapt higher I went to pull the curtains aside and pressed my face against the window.

"A foot-and-a-half and rising," I reported, not that I could see all that much through whirling snow so thick it might have been a cave wall hollowed out by the heat of our bodies.

"Maybe we'll have to tunnel out," she said. "When I was a kid we used to dig dens and forts under the snow banks."

Her warmth welcomed me back under the blankets. "I've waited out storms in snow caves a time or two in the mountains," I said, "but this is a whole lot nicer."

"It had better be." She snuggled deliciously closer. "You've got me. And the fire. And plenty to eat."

"Are you sure? I'd better check." My hand parted her thighs to stroke and probe until my fingers were slippery with her responsive wetness. By the time I raised them to my mouth for a taste she was working her own fingers into me with serious intent.

"Mm, yes," she said, sampling the glistening results. "Done just the way I like it." And suddenly she was burrowing under the blankets in a sudden assault on my eager cunt and clit, licking and sucking in a frenzy matched by the bucking of my hips. I had no chance to savor the delicious sensations, to let the tension build; my response came fast, hard, and out of control, leaving me quivering and totally, blissfully, wrung out.

As Lea untangled the blankets and pulled them back over us she said, with the satisfaction of a job well done, "Well, if there were any pristine, unmarked bits of these sheets left before this, there certainly aren't now." And she snuggled up against me with a soft sigh of contentment.

The next thing I knew, the white light of a snowy morning was seeping through the curtains. Lea lay sleeping soundly. A tremor stirred her eyelids; I wondered what she saw behind them, and how their tender skin might feel beneath my lips.

Her face was pale, but a faint flush lit the strong, lovely arch of her cheekbones. Her mouth, slightly swollen, was a deeper pink, tempting me to put out my tongue to taste myself there. I resisted, not wanting to wake her yet. Without interrupting the even pattern of her breathing, I edged out of the blankets and dressed in the back hallway. Then I filled old water jugs with sunflower and thistle seeds for the birds, and stepped outside.

At least two feet of snow lay on the flat, more in drifts, but it was coming down only lightly now. As I forged my way to the bird feeders, eager juncos and chickadees were already making forays from the shrubbery. Back at the porch I grabbed a shovel and cleared a path to my pickup truck, moving the snow in layers. The road hadn't been plowed yet, which was all right with me; what could be finer than being snow-bound with Lea? I contemplated the absurd mushroom of snow on the roof of the truck and decided to preserve it for a while as a natural work of art.

I went back to the house with a childlike urge to show Lea the birds, the snow, the slashes of blue sky emerging between the clouds; to share every small pleasure. Just savor the moment, I ordered myself. Don't complicate things. I shook my head, brushed as much snow as I could from my sweater and jeans, and concentrated on the joys of the present.

As soon as the warm inside air hit me, I knew Lea wasn't still curled up waiting under the covers. Regret was muted by my stomach's response to the smell of breakfast cooking.

"I hope you like French toast," she said, flipping the slices in a big frying pan on the woodstove. A pan of maple syrup was heating near the edge. "Not only have I had my way with your fire, I've ravaged your kitchen."

"Feel free to ravage anything you like," I said, admiring her outfit, which consisted entirely of wool socks and one of my old shirts, strategically unbuttoned.

"Which would you prefer, ravishment or eating?" She held me at arm's length with the spatula, then tugged at my belt just enough to let a little of the snow clinging to my sweater descend into where I was warmest. I yelped, but managed to stay on topic. "I can go either way." Which, of course, she must have known by then.

"I think I'd better keep my strength up," she said, flipping food onto plates, carrying them to the table, and digging right in. My stomach growled. I leaned over to kiss her, licking syrup from the sticky corners of her mouth. Laughter interspersed with kisses set the mood for the rest of the day. Something about being snowbound sets the inner kid free.

After we'd eaten breakfast and hauled in buckets and kettles of snow to melt for water, we worked together on shoveling the driveway. A few snowball volleys were exchanged, a few frosty fingers warmed in moist tender places, making them all the warmer and moister for the cool touch.

Then, when we'd cleared all the way to the still-unplowed road and worked up a fine sweat, Lea climbed up onto the back of the truck and surveyed the enclosed expanse of virgin white. "Snow angel time," she announced.

"There isn't room to spread your arms," I pointed out, but she just grinned and started unzipping her jacket.

"Okay, snow demon, then, if you're going to be picky." Off came jacket, shirt, bra; I watched in awe as she dropped even her trousers and flopped forward into the soft snow, arms curved upward and hands curling out from the top of her head like little crescent horns.

"Terrific!" I said, applauding. "How long do you want to stay there? Incidentally, I hear the plow coming."

"Help!" she spluttered through a mouthful of snow.

I managed to get her up without damaging too much of the very interesting impression she'd made in the snow. Even her cold-puckered nipples had left their marks. Then I half-dragged, half-carried her into the house and dumped her on the futon just as the plow approached. While she struggled to kick off her boots and the pants twisted around her ankles, I grabbed the pan of thickened maple syrup still hot on the edge of the stove.

Sugar-on-snow is a classic tradition in northern New England. I knew just what newly-imprinted snow I could use as a mold. When I came back inside with my sweet creations, Lea rolled around in helpless laughter once she realized what I'd done.

"You can have one of these if you want it." I held out the plate. "Haven't you sometimes kinda wished you could suck on your own tit?" I bent to lick one sweet, vaguely breast-shaped treat.

She eyed the rubbery forms beginning to lose definition in the warm air. "That wouldn't be my first choice. But if I'm not going to get a better offer, I'll fend for myself." She tossed off the blankets and arched her body upwards. Before I could get rid of the plate and follow my impulse to lay a trail of sticky kisses from her tender belly to her cunt, she had pulled up her pants and rolled off the bed.

"Wait a minute," I pleaded. "You can have anything you want!"

"What I want now is lunch," she said, rooting around on my

pantry shelves and choosing a few cans. "Don't interrupt while I'm in domestic mode."

My major hunger was situated well south of my stomach, but I cleaned off the syrup with snow-water as well as I could and kept out of her way. She was still shirtless; I enjoyed the scenery, the brisk grace of arms and hands, the subtle dancing movements of naked breasts.

The savory aroma of her concoction reminded me that I'd used a lot of energy shoveling. Food might not be all that bad an idea. I consumed my share of a soup somewhere between chili and mine-strone, and then asked, hopefully, "Apricots for dessert?"

Lea glanced down at herself. A faint flush spread across her skin as her nipples hardened into exquisitely tempting tongue-candy, but she pushed away from the table and grabbed a shirt. "That," she said, "might be better tonight by firelight. And anyway, there's still snow to clear, where the plow shoved it into the driveway." She scooped up her boots and shirt and headed toward the door, slip-ping her hand briefly but effectively between my thighs as she passed. "Plenty of time to build up tension."

So she was planning to stay at least another night. My tension hit levels even shoveling couldn't release.

The plow had left a huge bank of snow across the driveway. We cleared away most of it, leaving a narrow strip along the road by mutual consent to signify that we were still "snowed in." Then there were other paths to be cleared, to the woodpile and tool shed, and looming mounds to be raked from the eaves of the house. Finally, after consulting with my knees and deciding that a little more wouldn't make much difference, I strapped on snowshoes and went along the ski trail for a mile or so to check for fallen trees—and to give Lea a chance to rest.

When I came back through the dusk, lights were visible down the river valley. My nearest neighbors, at least, had their electricity back, and my house must have it too. I figured Lea would be cook-ing in the kitchen now, free to use the modest amenities of modern life it offered, but she was still tending to a kettle on the woodstove, and the cabin was lit only by the fire and an oil lamp I always kept handy on the mantle. I could see that the electric wall clock was run-ning and had been re-set, so Lea must be deliberately prolonging our adventure.

The soft light made the room seem all the warmer, more intimate, although Lea's presence cast the warmest glow. Something spicy was cooking, and there was still a lingering scent of maple syrup. Or—wasn't that the syrup pan heating again on the edge of the stove?

"What are we having?" I asked, trying to warm my frosty hands by the fire before daring to touch Lea.

"You'll see, when it's ready," she said, "but first you'll have to earn it by providing an appetizer."

"I'm all for that!" I leaned close to kiss her, and she responded with enthusiasm, but broke off too soon.

"That's fine, but not all I had in mind. You'll have to forage for it." She handed me the jacket I'd just hung on a peg by the door. "Bring me a basin of the whitest, most pristine snow."

I grinned, snatched another kiss, and got right to it. Her general plan was clear, although she'd certainly aroused my curiosity as to just how it was going to take shape.

When I returned, Lea stood for a moment, long-handled pan in hand, surveying the smooth white surface I'd provided. "Y'know," she said thoughtfully, "some folks say the only thing men can do that women can't is write their names in the snow standing up. Although you certainly wouldn't want to eat that yellow snow afterward." With deft, swift movements she poured a thin stream of hot syrup in curving lines onto the snow. The heart shape was only slightly lopsided, and the names "Kit" and "Lea" within were clearly distinguishable to an eye eager to see them.

"It's too beautiful to lift out and eat," I said in awe.

"You're right," Lea agreed. "And that wasn't my original plan, anyway. How about taking it out on the porch and letting it freeze? And then you can bring me some fresh snow."

I was back in minutes, warmed by a tingle of anticipation, becoming even warmer when I saw Lea waiting, entirely naked, with the lamp dimmed and the firelight caressing her curves.

"You didn't think you were going to get off without some very chilly personal contact, did you, Kit?" she said, trying to sound severe. "Put your hand in it. No, not there! In the snow!"

So I did, without flinching, and held it there, fingers spread, until Lea pulled me away. Silently, steadily, she poured a thick stream of amber syrup into the mold I had left.

"Now," she said, "you may warm your hand anywhere you'd like—" Her voice rose at least an octave as I took her up on the offer. She tightened her warm thighs around my fist, though, even while she reached into the basin of snow to lift out the congealed shape there and raise it to her lips.

"So tasty . . . " She nibbled at each distinct finger before drawing it all over her chin and throat and breasts, and lower. I sucked at her irresistible lips until she urged my mouth downward, and then I followed the sticky pathway to find the truest, warmest sweetness, and make it flow.

Dessert came first that night, complete with the savoring of apricots; the main dish never did get that much attention. Lea had to leave the next day, to tend to the other aspects of her life, but a few weeks later, when the maple sap was rising, she was back to sample a new crop of syrup.

Soon summer will be on us, with wild strawberries gleaming red in clearings along the trails. I'm sure we'll think of some way to incorporate the tangy intensity of their flavor with our own, but I doubt that anything will ever warm us more than sugar on snow. Fortunately, winter too will come again.

Just Like Candy
by Michele Zipp

It was cherry. I tasted its sweetness as I sucked, slowly, intently, holding the base with one hand. My mouth was salivating and my tongue swirled on the red tip, which seemed to glisten more and more each time it exited my mouth. The cherry-flavored delight filled my mouth, hot and wet and wanting more.

I remember when I was a young girl; the candy store was a block from my house. They just don't have shops like that anymore. The owner knew all the kids by name, and he even remembered what candies we preferred. They had every sugar imaginable, in every form there could possibly be from soft chewy bites to rock hard sticks of pure sugar—pure delight for a candy lover. It would be an excursion, once a week; we would set out to find the newest sweets, with the most intense flavor. The desire for candy as a child is like the lust for sex as an adult. It's craved, it satiates, it even calms.

It became clear very early on that I preferred the red candies. That particular store owner even called me Red. And as a girl, you either wanted the red candy all the time or you chose something like green to avoid any candy conundrum. I was always up for the challenge. I chose red. It was the taste of cherry that I wanted, and I was ready to fight for the red piece of candy when presented with a bag full of suckers. Why substitute when I knew what I wanted?

Picking the red candy is similar to always wanting to be the red game piece. To this day, whenever I have to choose which token to represent myself on a game board, I choose the red one.

When I was a teenager, my first car was red. It was an old Volkswagen Fox, which I don't think they even make anymore. But it was cute and small, and a five-speed (I always believed that automatic cars were for pussies). Best of all, it was cherry red. I've read that red cars get the most speeding tickets.

But with sweets . . . it almost didn't matter if it was a piece of hard candy. Almost. Just like it almost didn't matter if the red candy tasted more like watermelon than cherry. But I said almost. The taste of cherry was my favorite pleasure. And I did take the most delight in lollipops. There was always something about the sucking that I especially liked. It was my oral fixation and this was one childhood indulgence that I was not going to sacrifice. Playfulness is one of the keys to youthfulness. I particularly loved the lollipop with the surprise when you got to the core, the soft chewy center. Thinking of it makes my mouth water to this day. In fact, thinking of it right now causes a surge of desire in my mouth much like the billow of want I feel when thinking about sex. I would work so hard sucking to get to it—the prize. There are some things I would do anything for.

Red is a powerful color. When a woman wears red lipstick, her  lips are commanding attention—and they get it. A woman can accentuate the part of her body that she wants you to notice first—it may even be the first part she wants you to feel. As you kiss, the red pigment of her lipstick smears a trace; your hands may be in her hair, pulling gently downward. But it all started with the kiss. The lure of the red of the lips. Red is desire, lust, passion, love, and the color of the loss of innocence.

Now, as it was then, I love Halloween. As adults, we dress up, go to parties, role-play, and have a few cocktails. Some Cabernet perhaps, a cranberry and vodka, champagne with a splash of Chambord—red drinks, drinks that taste like candy. And if we are lucky and if it's a proper Halloween party, there's even some candy to suck on. Perversions. And what woman hasn't been some sort of vampiress on October 31st? There's something about blood that is really sexy. Vampire movies are full of vile innuendoes and we indulge in their every fantasy. Why else has biting and spanking made its way into foreplay?

I love it when a man softly bites on my neck, sucking even, pulling the blood to the surface. Or if he sucks on my toes, which of course are almost always painted red. There is this color, Cherries in the Snow, that is the perfect shade of red, and there is not much that's sexier than the sight of my perfectly pedicured cherry toe coming out my lover's mouth. That is, I thought nothing was sexier, until I first saw him, sucking on a red lollipop. Foreplay of the very visual variety.

It was a typical winter day. The sky was darker than it should have been for the afternoon because of a storm that was rolling in.

There was a biting chill in the wind, and the air was crisp. You could see your breath as you exhaled. I had just walked out of the store on the corner by my apartment. I went in to buy a newspaper so I had something to read while I was on the train. At the checkout, I saw a bin filled with lollipops, the ones with bubblegum in the center. I picked cherry, paid, and left.

I had my own candy that day and was waiting for the light to change to cross the street to catch my train. I had unwrapped the round cherry lollipop from its wrapper and could instantly smell the sweet scent of its sugar. It was cold when I first put it into my hot, wet mouth, just like my fingers were when they hit the cold air. I had to remove my glove to take the candy out of its wrapper. But quickly the hard candy warmed in my mouth and the juice of the cherry was flavoring my tongue. My fingers were also safely back in the warmth of my mitten.

He was on the opposite side of the road, wearing a black wool jacket. I could see a hint of his red sweater peeking out at the top. He was tall, over six feet, and wearing dark denim pants and gray shoes. His hair was mostly hidden under his dark wool hat, but I could tell that his locks were a dark chocolate brown from the few curls that peeked out from under his hat. I watched him suck what appeared to be a red lollipop, much like the one I was sucking on, from across the street. I could tell he was enjoying it by the focused look he had on his face, but I did notice he became distracted . . . by me, on the opposite side of the street, sucking on a red lollipop. It seemed like he was looking at me as the cars passed before us, watching as my tongue swirled around the cherry tip of my candy. Just like his tongue was intently lavishing his own. I imagined it was my toe in his mouth—a prelude to before he got my real cherry.

When the traffic light changed to red, we walked toward each other. It was like our movements were synchronized. I felt his eyes on mine, then his eyes on the lollipop dancing in and out from between my lips, as his went in and out of his mouth, mimicking mine.

I noticed his eyes as he got closer. They were blue and they were fixed on me. I saw the cherry lollipop slowly come out of his mouth, his glistening lips moistened by the candy. It was like I could smell the sweet cordial scent coming toward me like he was moving in for a kiss. His lips were full and tinted from the red of his lollipop. I thought of what they would feel like when they touched mine. I imagined them to be sticky sweet. And when his red tongue would slide into my mouth, I would finally taste the exact flavor of what he had been sucking.

Eve tempted Adam with the apple. Why couldn't he tempt me with his lollipop?

I could feel my face getting hotter despite the cold. I knew the blood was rushing to my cheeks, making me flush, making my lips redder, my insides warmer. It wasn't only my lollipop that was making my mouth salivate—it was him. The thought of unzipping his coat, unbuttoning his red shirt, pulling his T-shirt up over his head, feeling his chest, kissing his neck, biting his flesh as I moved down. It was like I could feel his cherry-scented breath hot on my neck as he undressed me. He would start with my gloves, pulling them off with his teeth, then sucking on my fingers. My hands would wander to his head, and I would remove his hat and run my hands through his hair. He would start to lick me at the nape of my neck, just like he licked the lollipop, slowly and softly. I would feel his fingers fidgeting with the buttons of my coat, then with my shirt. Once naked, he would move his hands up to my shoulders, but his tongue would move down, and he would suck on my nipple ever so gently, moving further downward to get to my core, his reward, my candy.

I would want to taste him so badly, but I would wait. Wait to nibble on his ear first. Then, experiencing the feel of his nipple in my mouth, swirling my tongue around its reddish tip, descending to his hardening cock, which my hands found moments before my mouth would. I would take the base in my hand and pull down, making him harder, and bring my red lips to his tip, licking my way around the head, wanting more and more of him as my mouth salivated. I would feel a throbbing yearn to have him inside me, his tongue inside my mouth. I bet he would taste just like he smelled—just like my candy, my cherry lollipop.

Forbidden Fruit and Honey
by Salome Wilde

She sliced the apple deftly, small knife held tightly in her slender olive-skinned fingers. Though he might have been afraid at the thought of giving the seductive creature a weapon—even so harmless a tool as this small fruit knife—he did not hesitate a moment when she asked for it. Certainly, there was risk; she was Gallic and her people still resisted the Emperor's will. Yet, though older than he liked them, she came highly recommended by several of the foot soldiers in his legion, and she was clearly well trained to serve. More: an agile maturity and quiet dignity in bearing told him she could be trusted. The young Roman officer smiled to himself as she quickly and efficiently cored the ripe golden fruit. He had been

wrong in the past in placing his confidence too quickly in beautiful distractions, but he was wiser now, if little older. He remembered the young man who took all of his gold one long drunken winter night at a lonely outpost. His smile broadened.

Let me always live a little dangerously, he thought, pridefully, remembering the lad's ripe lips and tight nether hole. Not skilled but eager, that one. He wondered how the clever wretch spent his coins.

She was now carving the fruit into eight neat wedges. Certainly, being fed was a treat, but he felt his erection begin to wilt as he wondered if she would be simply and predictably servile. The procurer he paid, a shrewd but humble businessman who spoke several languages, made plain that the officer was to enjoy whatever pleased him with the buxom, chestnut-haired woman. There was only one limitation: she did not speak his language. That was no problem for the soldier, who could have little to say to a whore of any land. No, he had been long away from female flesh, and it was not words but flesh that he craved.

He lay back on his elbow, exposing his semi-rigid state to her gaze. Let his body language tell her that it would take more than borrowed knives and apples to arouse his hunger. And, of course, if such hints did not produce desirable results, he could easily lay claim to the satin rope that fastened about her waist to hold the sheer gown around her and bind her busy hands overhead. His cock bobbed and began to rise again as he thought of how good it would be to release some of his pent-up energies on her ample derrière. He longed for battle and glory but had found only waiting and ever more waiting as his battalion advanced across the frontiers of Gaul, a foreign land that was little different from his own but for language and cuisine. A combination of too little combat and equally little exotic escape left him more than restless. Hence, as he looked at the whore before him, he wished her skin were not so close in color to his own, her eyes a lighter—or darker—hue, her figure less like that of so many other women he had lain with, if less youthful and taut. He considered the pleasures he might find in plying his belt to that rounded rump, but hesitated.

She had bathed him well, he admitted to himself. Those nimble fingers worked the knots out of his shoulders and flanks as he soaked in the hot, fragrant water of a luxurious tub. When he turned to her to ask if she found him attractive—certainly, being overripe in years, she must be used to a lesser quality of man, she raised her eyebrows and showed she did not understand. He would have preferred a purred gush of adoration, but her silence, too, was good. It offered a sweet tribute to his power, he thought.

The whore must have noticed his cock flagging, for she had come, apple in hand, to his side. First, she licked the blade slowly and carefully with a rich, velvet tongue and placed it beside him. That she tasted the fruit's juices, in this way assuring him that it was not poisoned, and he could relax, images of teasing and torturing her with the knife's edge flickering before him. This idea was quickly dismissed, though, as she dropped all the pieces of fruit at once into his hands. Surprised that she was not going to feed him, he quirked an eyebrow at her as he took the slices and she, boldly holding his gaze for a moment, smiled. She moved to stand over him and raised her short gown, then brought her hands down to spread her plump labia, richly covered in coffee-hued curls. She looked down at the apples in his hands from over the tops of full, round breasts, then looked down between her legs. He

saw the dew that moistened her and relished her arousal. Too many times had he lain with serviceable but unfeeling women. He hardened fully again as he dropped the apples beside him and brought his fingers up to plumb those moist depths.

She reached out to stay his hand. Shocked at this unexpected insolence, the officer responded instinctively. He caught her wrist and held it hard as he began to rise. She winced, frustration in her heavy-lidded eyes. It was clear she wanted to speak but would not. Her mute impotence reached him. He came to his feet, took her chin in his hand, and looked deeply into her eyes. They were hazel, flecked with brown, the lids dark but not painted, the lashes thick. "Why so willful all of a sudden?" he said, loosening his grip.

She understood exactly what he asked, understood every word he had said from the moment he was in her presence, bargaining for her favors as if her lack of Roman citizenship and her age made her worthless, even as a prostitute. She knew well that his eager but under-endowed underlings had sung her praises; she had worked magic on their tired bodies and lonely minds in order to lure this one to her. A fine feather in her cap this officer would be.

She basked in the further pleasure of how quickly she had turned him from antagonism to sympathy. How she enjoyed this moment, the rush of pleasure when such strong, determined men grew interested in what a whore was thinking. Keeping silent always brought the change quickly. So hurried were these young men of war, not yet wise enough to know when to lie back and be served, unlikely to live long enough to reach such maturity. This one especially. She fought the urge to shake her head at him as she had fought the urge to speak; either would have ruined her plan for his temptation. Winning the little battle with herself, she made a show of lowering her eyes, then took his hand with great gentleness. He allowed it. Good. She brought her lips to his wrist and kissed it warmly. He let out a heavy breath. Better. She bent to retrieve a few of the fallen pieces of apple and placed them again in his outstretched hand. He tensed but took them. Then, she brought him to be seated once more on the furred floor. He rested on his elbow, apples held out for whatever purpose she had in mind. Still impatient for action, however, he reached over with his empty hand and firmly squeezed her right breast, rubbing his thumb across a stiffening nipple. She leaned into his embrace, pretending to enjoy the warmth of his hand when it was the fact that he held the apples just as she wished that pleased her. How delicious was this dance of power, even when she alone knew it was, indeed, a dance.

Bending to his side, she used her teeth to take a slice of the fruit from his curved palm. When she sat up again, he pulled her to him by her breast, and she grinned as she saw that his cock was once more at full attention. Holding the apple carefully, she brought it from her mouth to his, and he immediately sank his teeth into it, snapping it neatly in half. He sought her gaze then and she gave it to him, watching him chew, then return to her mouth for more. He released her breast and leaned in to her. She maneuvered the tidbit so he might take the rest, and when he did so, she parted her lips and gave her mouth up to be devoured as well. The pulp and sweet juice moved between them as he kissed her hungrily. The kiss was overly rough, uninspired. She sighed, and was certain by his increased vigor that he'd mistaken her reaction for arousal. So be it: arousal came in many forms, and her excitement at her control of this potentially violent man was palpable.

When he broke the embrace to swallow, she licked her lips and swallowed too, then dipped down to his palm again, retrieved another slice, and this time nudged the back of the empty hand he was leaning on. He warmed immediately to her mute, pet-like display. He sat back and she dropped the wedge gently into his palm. Then, she leaned back and, once more, parted her curls to expose her sex. He smiled broadly, finally having grasped her purpose. He took the apple and dipped it inside her, stroking the pink opening that glistened in the candlelight, which she held wide in graceful fingers. The flesh of the fruit was firm and cool against her soft folds, and she enjoyed his small thrusts. But soon he grew gentler, caressing her with soft swirling strokes that drew forth generous moisture. A soft honeyed scent drifted up to lightly woo their senses.

With more care than she would have credited him, he softly withdrew the fruit and brought it to his lips. Before it entered his mouth, however, her lips had parted, too, and she inclined her head softly forward. He took her enthusiasm as a sign that she was as hungry as he for a taste of her. Surprisingly, this apparent selfishness pleased him, and, with a warm yet smug expression, he brought the apple to her ripe mouth and rubbed it back and forth across her lips. She tensed, holding very still, and let her eyes close.

When he bent down to coat the slice again with her honey, she quickly and adroitly wiped her lips clean with the back of her hand, then rubbed the wetness into the fur beneath her. As she did so, she held herself open with her other hand and sighed warmly at his tender attentions.

At last he brought the apple slice to his lips and bit it with a satisfying crunch. "I have never been more fond of dessert," he murmured as he reached for more fruit, never taking his eyes off her sex. "Such a delectable—"

His words were cut off by the closing of his throat. The poison with which she had coated her vulva could not harm her through those tissues, but it worked swiftly and surely when swallowed. The officer reached out for her, then fell to the floor at her feet. Did he, even in that last moment, mistake her for an ally? Or had his last breath brought him the knowledge that the taste of forbidden fruit, however sweet it may seem, is, in the end, most bitter?

Other Girls
by R. Gay

Zed loved and hated working for Barnaby's Traveling Carnival of Wonders. The days and nights were long—spent in a cramped, poorly constructed space with fryers and spinning bins selling twelve flavors of cotton candy and funnel cakes. He lived alone in his trailer, traveling across back roads through the Midwest with the human curiosities of the carnival—a fat lady, gypsy fortune teller, tattooed men and women, a guy with 96 piercings, some second-rate clowns, and the miscreant carnies that handled most of the midway attractions. Night after night, Zed endured grease burns, rude customers, the sharp treble of calliope music and the broken PA system Barnaby used to shill tickets to the Wonder Tent. He kept to himself, paid Barnaby his cut and figured that the life he lived was as good as any.

What Zed loved was the small town girls with their unfortunate makeup choices, acid wash denim mini skirts, white pleather boots, and false innocence. He loved how their hair smelled of Aqua Net and that they spoke a language formed by wanderers and television—not quite current but not left behind. There was no pretense with these girls. They knew he was in no position to take them away or change their lives. They had no expectations of him beyond what he could offer for an hour or two on the worn couch of his trailer or in an abandoned barn or in the back of a father's pickup truck. They were hungry and angry and simple and complicated and the most beautiful creatures Zed had ever met. He often wondered what they saw in him. He was handsome, he knew, and he had a decent body. The long hours and labor of his work saw to that. But beyond a quick smile and smooth line, Zed knew that if he ever stuck around, his small town girls would soon tire of him.

In Topeka, Kansas, there was Jenny, who stuck her bubble gum behind her left ear as she sat on a hay bale and sucked his cock. Afterward, she wiped her lower lip with her thumb, tucked Zed back into his jeans and returned to the midway with her friends. In Grand Island, Nebraska, Zed met Wendy, who played hard to get, showing up at his booth for a funnel cake drizzled with honey. He slid the greasy paper plate toward her and slowly, she began to unravel the cake, first licking the honey, then dangling long pieces of fried dough above her mouth and slowly nibbling tiny morsels. An hour later, Wendy returned for Sassy Apple cotton candy. She stood a few feet away, ignoring the crowds milling around her, as she leaned against the side of the lemonade stand, twirling her fingers through the green wisps of spun sugar, pulling strands to her mouth and letting them dissolve on her tongue. She stood there for an hour. She never stopped staring at Zed.

Later that night, after the carnival had closed, after Zed had finished cleaning and restocking his booth and he was shooting the shit with Trent, the guy with 96 piercings, Wendy walked on by. He could smell her perfume—Charlie Red—before he saw her, and then she was standing in front of him, staring at Zed, hands on her hips. She cocked her head over her shoulder and started walking away. Zed shrugged, flashed Trent a toothy grin and followed. He followed Wendy past the silent Tilt-A-Whirl and the Tornado until they reached the Ferris Wheel. She pushed him into an empty car waiting for a passenger and it began to swing as he fell onto the white metal bench. She giggled, started unzipping his jeans. She lifted her pink skirt, and shimmed out of her panties, gently pushing them into his shirt pocket. She kissed his neck and his collarbone and dragged her tongue down his muscled chest. Then she straddled him, hot and wet, her thigh muscles straining, the bench swinging faster and farther as she rode Zed until she was satisfied.

Each July, Barnaby's Traveling Carnival of Wonders spent two weeks in East Texas. It was a locale everyone hated. Over several years, the carnies had developed the saying, "Nothing good ever comes from spending too much time in East Texas," but Barnaby insisted on going. It was a cash cow, he would say to anyone who would listen, what with so many people so hard up for a little entertainment. For Zed, it was an ungodly kind of hot, dust always blowing everywhere, the sun relentless. The days were miserable and in the late afternoons, when the sun was the hottest, Zed could barely breathe in his booth. On the first Wednesday of the carnival's stay, Zed burned his left forearm when he didn't back away from the funnel cake fryer in time, after dropping a fresh ring of batter.

Cussing loudly, Zed hopped from foot to foot, called for help, and was soon speeding along a two-lane highway to the nearest hospital as his arm blistered into a fiery red. The nurse who cleaned the burn and wrapped the wound in gauze was named Sadie. She wore purple scrubs and matching purple sneakers. She talked with a thick drawl. She held his hand a little too long as she finished with him and she scrawled her phone number with a felt tip pen on his good hand.

That night, as Zed lay in his trailer, staring at the ceiling, feeling sorry for himself and drinking a lukewarm beer, there was a light knock at the door. He sat up too quickly, banging his head against the shelf just above his bed. "Come in," he growled. The door opened and Sadie smiled before stepping into his trailer. She looked around, wrinkling her nose slightly as she took in the cramped quarters, the two burner stove, the small worn couch covered with stained t-shirts and wrinkled pairs of jeans. As she crossed the short distance to where Zed sat, she dragged one finger along the galley counter. "So this is where a carny lives?" she drawled. Zed nodded, slid to the edge of his bed and patted the empty space next to him. "And this is where a carny sleeps."

Sadie stopped and stepped out of her scrubs. She had a beautiful, tan body, with ample curves and an odd-looking birthmark just below her navel. "I'm here for a follow up visit," she said. She took a swig of beer from the bottle in Zed's hand and returned it to him. Zed smiled, as he was wont to do in such situations, and offered his injured arm for inspection. Sadie gently kissed the gauze, then dragged her lips up Zed's arm to his neck. As she straddled his lap, she slid her tongue between his lips. He liked the taste of her mouth—slightly sour and cool. He rolled Sadie onto her stomach, and traced the length of her spine with his beer bottle. He kissed the undersides of her ass, parting her legs. As he slid his cock inside her, Sadie sighed. "I've been waiting for this all day," she said softly. Later, as they lay against each other, their sweat lingering in the humid night air, she told him that he tasted like powdered sugar.

In the morning, Zed splashed water on his face and changed into fresh jeans and a t-shirt. Sadie was gone, only a pair of rubber gloves left next to her pillow proving she had ever been there. He rubbed the stubble across his jaw and stepped out of his trailer, squinting in the late morning sun. Around him, the other carnies were setting up their wares, heating up fryers, squeezing lemons. Trent was stretching for his show. Barnaby was chasing after one of the non-Siamese twins that he passed off as the real thing. It was a normal, albeit hot day in East Texas, with far too many left for his liking. And then, from the corner of his eye, Zed saw a woman, close to him in age, he guessed, with jet black hair, wearing a faded metal band tank top and cut off jean shorts. She had one hand over her eyes as she scanned the activity around her, and the other hand on her slender hips. As she walked by Zed's trailer, he couldn't help but stare. She walked with confidence. She knew where she was going. She wanted something. She was not at all like most small town girls. He had no idea how he knew this, but he was certain it was true.

Later, as the sun began to set, there was a line of clamoring customers, seven people deep, and he could feel spun sugar sinking into his skin. As he handed a young couple two bags of strawberry cotton candy, Zed saw the woman again. She was standing a few customers back, waiting her turn, crisp dollar bills in her hand. When she reached the counter, Zed leaned toward her, flashing his brightest smile.

"What can I do you for?"

"Not much, I'm sure," the woman said. "But in the meantime, I'll take some cherry cotton candy."

Zed cocked his head to the right, then turned around to the spinning bins, holding the paper rod as he spun the sugar in soft strands until he had made a veritable tower of confection. When he turned around, he tried his brightest smile again. The woman regarded him with indifference. She didn't even flinch when Zed tried to brush the palm of her hand as he took her money. She flicked her tongue forward and began pulling cotton candy into her mouth, then reached for the handle. She stood there, ignoring the complaints of the growing line behind her, and ate every last strand of candy with a voracious appetite. Zed marveled at her, and from this close vantage point, was able to see a tattoo of a rose creeping up from beneath the scooped neck of her tank top.

"Is that the Yellow Rose of Texas?" he asked, pointing to her neckline.

"I'll take another one," she said.

Zed spun another batch of cotton candy for his customer. This time, when the woman reached for the candy, Zed pulled it back. "This one will only cost you your name." She rolled her eyes, looked as if she was giving the matter serious contemplation. "You can call me Rose," she finally said.

Zed handed Rose her candy. "As much as I'd like to continue this, I have a lot to do," he said, motioning to the long line behind her. Rose didn't look back. She continued eating her candy, more slowly this time.

"Not bad, though I suppose it would be rather difficult to make a mess of this sort of thing."

Zed shrugged. "You're not far from the truth. Why don't you come by later?"

Rose took a handful of napkins from the dispenser on the counter. "Just so you understand—I'm not like other girls."

"That's what they all say," Zed called out as Rose walked away.

He spent the rest of the evening pondering the extent of Rose's rose tattoo and the flavors of cotton candy he could spin for her. He daydreamed about the slight gap between her two front teeth and the faint scar he noticed just below her lower lip. He ignored the heat, the grease, the aching muscles in his arms, the sweaty gauze and the irritation of his burn. After the carnival closed, he cleaned his booth with an efficiency he didn't know he possessed. Then, he waited. And waited. But Rose never came. Later, in his trailer, which he cleaned, thoroughly, for the first time in months, Zed thought about cooking Rose dinner, all so he could learn the story of the sharpness of her tongue. Early the next morning, he shaved, scrounged for a clean outfit, and opened his booth before noon, despite the fact that there was only a trickle of carnival-goers.

Rose didn't return for three days. When she did, she wore faded jeans, with the knees missing and a sizable hole where a back pocket used to be. She also wore a bikini top that showed off a finely muscled abdomen that Zed yearned to touch and a keloided scar where he imagined her appendix once was.

"I thought I would see you the other night."

"I told you I'm not like other girls," Rose said.

He nodded toward her scar. "You're not much for covering things up, are you?"

"I don't see no call for that sort of thing. Can I get some cotton candy now?"

"What flavor can I do you for?"

"Surprise me," Rose said.

Zed poured a combination of cherry and vanilla dust into his spinning bin and waited for the machine to work its magic. Then, carefully, he worked paper around the bin, collecting red and white strands until he had created a feather concoction he hoped Rose would enjoy. "This one's on the house," he said as he passed the cotton candy to Rose. "And I would really like to see you later. No strings attached."

"There are always strings."

Zed thought about those words, about strings and attachments and the fact that he had none. Such things had never bothered him before. Now, some strange, dark-haired woman he knew nothing about, beyond the truths her body shared, had him thinking all kinds of things. Rose returned several times throughout the day, and each time, Zed spun her elaborate combinations of cotton candy, trying to outdo himself with each effort. As he handed her his last creation, a heady combination of grape, strawberry and orange cotton candy, Rose actually cracked a smile, her cheeks arching slightly, her lips never parting. "I'll see you later," she said, as she sampled the candy, walking away slowly.

In the early hours of the morning, after most of the carnies and their conquests had fallen asleep, Zed heard his trailer door open. He lay across his freshly made bed, listening to music in white cotton boxers and bare feet. Rose crawled over his body to the other side. She lay in the crook of his arm, resting one hand across his stomach, tucking her long fingers just beneath the waist of Zed's boxers. She started telling him about herself—where she was born, how she had ended up in East Texas, the many different ways in which she was not like other girls. Zed hung on to every word, even after he could barely hold his eyes open and he caught himself spiraling toward sleep.

When she was done talking, she slid out of her jeans and panties and Zed lay between her thighs. He traced the raised scar across her belly. He kissed each of her inner thighs, then dragged his tongue upward, her scent stronger when he reached her cunt. He held her pussy lips apart with his fingers, and slowly, carefully, he began to lick her clit. Rose slid her fingers through Zed's thick hair. She stretched her long legs, wrapping them around his shoulders. Zed felt her clit swelling, and he wrapped his lips around it, suckling gently, then with more insistence. Rose was not shy. She cried out, then moaned, loudly. He slid his tongue lower, sampling the texture of the slick insides of her pussy lips. He knew, as he begin to slide his tongue in and out of her cunt, her thighs gripping tighter, her cries louder yet, that if he had to spend the rest of his life pleasuring Rose with his mouth, he would die a happy man.

Zed woke late the next afternoon to the smell of coffee and eggs. Rose stood in the kitchen wearing an apron he didn't recognize and nothing else. She leaned forward against the stove on one foot, the other tucked behind her knee. There was a look of concentration on her face as she sprinkled black pepper and Tabasco sauce into the frying pan. She looked in his direction and smiled. "We need to eat." Zed liked the sound of her words—the implication of mutual need. Shyly, he sat at the small linoleum table built for two.

"Is there anything I can do to help?"

Rose shook her head. "Just tell me how you like my cooking," she said, serving him a plateful of scrambled eggs.

Zed ate energetically. He couldn't remember the last time he'd enjoyed a good breakfast. Or good company. At the same time. Rose sat across from him, tangling her feet with his. She drank from a tall mug of coffee, black. Zed made a mental note. "I should be getting to work," he said, once he had finished, and rinsed their plates.

"I could use some work, myself," Rose said.

Instinctively, Zed cringed. But then he looked at Rose, and how beautiful she looked in his cramped trailer, and he recalled all of her stories. "I might be able to see about that," he finally said.

After they showered, Rose kissed him just behind his left ear, and told him she'd be back later. Zed watched her carefully, in case this was the last time he ever saw her. She came back an hour later, found him at his booth. She was carrying two large duffel bags and an old hat box. "Come on in and toss those in the corner," Zed told Rose. She slid into the booth and stood to the side as she watched Zed work—the deft manner in which he dropped batter into the fryers, the way he held his wrist as he spun sugar for the cotton candy.

"You didn't think I'd come back," she said, when there was a lull in the steady stream of business.

Zed frowned.

Rose placed two fingers over Zed's lips, sliding her other hand between their bodies to unbutton his jeans. "I told you I'm not like other girls."

Zed felt his cock stiffen, and he leaned against the counter, his back to the midway. Rose lowered his jeans around his ankles and kissed the tip of his cock, before pulling her own pants down. Zed turned their bodies around so that Rose was leaning against the counter. He opened her shirt, her full breasts falling into his hands, squeezing roughly. He quickly forgot about the carnival around them. His senses were overwhelmed by Rose and the sticky sweet stench of sugar and the heat of East Texas and her long fingers stroking his cock. He lowered his mouth to her nipples, pulling them into his mouth, nibbling softly with the edges of his teeth. Rose clasped the back of his neck, gently tugging the stray hairs. He slid his hands to her hips and squeezed, enjoying the sensation of holding her body. Zed lifted Rose off the floor and gasped as he slid his cock inside her.

He clenched his jaw, trying to control himself. He felt Rose's hot breath against his ear, her tongue against the lobe, her words against his neck. He kissed her, hard, trying to swallow her tongue, his fingers digging into her ass, where later, there would be bruises. He fucked her hard and slow, forgetting about all the small town girls who had come before. He could feel her thigh muscles gripping his waist. She muffled her moans by burying her face into his shoulder. She dug her fingernails into his back, rending the thin material of his t-shirt. When Rose came, she tossed her head back, smiling widely. Zed didn't allow himself to come. He wanted to save that for later. He waited until her body stopped shuddering, and her damp legs slid down his body. He waited until she straightened her clothes and wiped her forehead. Then, they worked side by side for the rest of the evening, Rose taking the opportunity to spin sugar around her fingers and have her fill of cotton candy. A week later, Zed didn't leave Rose behind when he and Barnaby's Traveling Carnival of Wonders left East Texas. She was, after all, nothing like other girls.

Cling
by Tenille Brown

After she turned thirty, Lynn Ford found there were certain things she could no longer hold on to. There was the silver belly ring she'd had since she was twenty-three, her bed full of stuffed animals—some she'd even had since childhood, but she was a grown woman now and it was time to move on.

Then there was Shawn.

Shawn Whitmore had been the last thing she'd parted with, and she found he was the most difficult thing to shake even though she knew it was for the best. They had established the ground rules early on. They would only see each other now and then. They would enjoy it for as long as it lasted and after, well, they would handle it like adults. She had given it six months—a year tops.

But two years later Shawn was still around and Lynn couldn't  figure out why. He wasn't exactly what you would call a boyfriend; he was simply a convenience she occasionally sought refuge in until something better came along, something real.

See, at her age, Lynn knew she needed something that would stick, something that would still be there when she was old and tired and the sex had gone stale. She needed someone she could talk to, someone who shared her interests, someone she could build a life with.

Yes, Lynn had her reasons for letting Shawn go, but laying alone in her bed now, sleepless at a quarter past one, it was hard to convince herself of any of them. Maybe Shawn was having second thoughts, too. If she was still thinking about him, wasn't it possible he missed her?

Her heart began to race.

Had he called? Had she fallen into such a deep sleep that she hadn't heard the phone?

Lynn fell back against the pillows, glanced at the answering machine and sighed. Of course he hadn't called. She'd told him not to.

And Shawn had obliged.

He hadn't called, hadn't come by, hadn't even asked her friends how she was doing for seventeen days. Seventeen *days*?

Had it really been that long?

She supposed it was possible. After all, it wasn't the days that bothered her. The days were easy. There was work and friends and things to clean or organize, but then it fell dark and everything went sexy, the music on the radio, the shows on television. It was harder to think clearly at night, harder not to reach for the phone, not to pick up her keys and drive to his place and tell him never mind, forget what she said. Forget it all.

And every night it was automatic, like a silent alarm that jolted her awake like clockwork at a quarter past one. The sheets were tangled, clinging to her damp skin, and she lay there alone, remembering how Shawn always called after work, after she had already been asleep for two hours. How he would have made it to her place by one and by a quarter past he would be in her bed, his arms around her, his lips on hers.

Maybe she shouldn't have fucked him that last time. Then she wouldn't be laying there thinking about what he wore the last time she saw him, what he smelled like, what he looked the like. The last words he said, the way he felt those last few moments he was inside her. Yes, that was where she went wrong.

But besides that, he was so fucking sweet, too sweet sometimes. He never had a bad word to say to her even when she was being a bitch. And on top of that he was sexy and charming and funny and he smelled nice all the time and she liked lying next to him even if they weren't fucking.

But she did like the fucking. Yes, the fucking was the best part and Lynn knew she would miss that the most. She would take days off from work to stay home and fuck him. She would cancel plans with friends, move appointments.

And all of that was fine when she was twenty-eight, twenty-nine even, but she was thirty now and there was her future to consider. Could she marry Shawn?

She couldn't and she knew it.

So why couldn't she just forget him?

Lynn glanced about the dark room. The answer was simple. Shawn was still there. His cologne still clung to her sheets, his pictures were still scattered around her apartment, his shoes still rested under her bed.

She had never gotten around to dropping it all off at his place. She didn't see the need. She didn't hate him, after all. And the break-up wasn't bitter. It was clean, cordial, the way it should have been.

So, she'd take it to him. That couldn't be so bad. She would pack it all up and drop it off at his door and it would be over. Lynn exhaled and crawled deeper under the covers. Yes, she'd wrap this thing up in a tidy little bow and that would be that, no muss, no fuss. She smiled, her face sank into her pillow and finally, at two forty-five, she slept.

Lynn gathered everything that reminded her of Shawn and tossed the items one by one into an empty box. The things that actually belonged to Shawn took up little space. It was those things he had managed to make his own that filled up the rest, like the glass he drank out of whenever he came over or the CDs that had played softly while they lay in bed or the sponge she always used to wash him when they showered together.

She picked up a wooden box that sat on the bar. She hesitated, flipping open the lid and peering inside. Lynn stared at the rows of salt water taffy. He had gotten the candy for her that weekend they spent at the beach, after she had gotten mad and they had argued.

She didn't even like taffy. It was too sweet and made her teeth hurt and it was so hard to get rid of even after you were done. It clung to the roof of your mouth for hours afterward. And if Shawn knew her at all, he would have known better than to think it would make her feel better.

But he went out and bought a box of it and sat on the edge of the bed and fed her a piece and it really wasn't that bad. In fact, it was quite good actually and she asked for another. He'd fed her one piece after another as she lay beside him in bed, letting her lick it off his fingers, suck it off his tongue until he had found his way beneath the covers with her and she had forgotten what it was she was mad about in the first place.

Lynn frowned and snapped the lid shut and tossed it into the box with the rest. She couldn't get distracted now. That was why she wouldn't call him first. She knew how that would go. Shawn would get her on the phone and he would take everything she said and twist it into something that no longer made sense and before she knew it she would be talking all soft and sweet and the frown would have fallen from her face and she would all of a sudden be whispering to him the many ways she wanted him to come fuck her.

No, she would just pack everything and take it over to him. She didn't care if he wasn't there when she got there. As a matter of fact, it would be better if he wasn't. That way she could just leave his things outside the door and be done with it.

Lynn scanned the apartment for anything she might have forgotten before she grabbed her keys off the hook by the door, and walked out.

Lynn balanced the box on her hip with one hand and knocked three times with the other. She straightened her t-shirt and pulled at her shorts. She was careful about what she wore, sure not to put on anything he had seen her in and commented on, nothing he had slipped over her head and tossed onto the floor.

She listened for footsteps, for the radio or the television, but heard nothing. She knocked three more times, then placed the box down on the welcome mat. He was probably in there with someone. That was why he hadn't called. He had found someone else, maybe there had always *been* someone else.

That would be better, she supposed. It would make it easier somehow if he were in there fucking the shit out of some other girl. Lynn turned and walked away.

But then the doorknob turned and the door creaked open and she heard his voice, low and raspy.

"Lynn?"

Lynn bit down on her bottom lip and forced her feet to keep moving.

"Lynn, stop."

She heard his feet hit the pavement, felt him walk up behind her. She halted but kept facing the street, afraid that if she turned around she'd melt.

"I was just dropping by a box of your stuff, Shawn," she said, forcing calm into her voice.

"You can't even look at me."

Lynn closed her eyes tight.

No, don't look at him. Don't look at the way his hair lay in soft, silky curls against his scalp. Don't look at the way his eyes look right through you, the way his lips curl up in that crooked smile of his. Don't look at that cleft in his chin and remember all the times you lay on his chest and stuck your finger there and smiled up at him.

But Lynn did it anyway.

And his skin was still that torturous shade of golden brown that looked kissed by the sun. He was shirtless, his bare chest tinged with the same knee-weakening glow as his arms and legs. His gym shorts lay snugly on his hips and brushed against his knees.

He pointed toward his door. "Look, do you want to come in or anything? I've got some lemonade. I could pour you a glass."

"I've got lemonade at home," Lynn said. She didn't really, but that wasn't the point. He was not getting her inside that apartment.

"Well, I just ran in from fooling around with my car so my hands are kind of messy. Could you at least bring the box in for me?" He held his hands up for her to see the oil stains on his palms.

Lynn looked at him long and hard, thought of just turning and walking away, but instead she said, "And that's all. I'm just bringing it in, dropping it on the counter and I'm leaving."

Shawn held his hands up in surrender. "Fine."

Lynn bent down to lift the box. Shawn's scent slipped effortlessly inside her nostrils. His shorts grazed her cheek. She cleared her throat and followed him inside.

Her eyes darted from corner to corner of the apartment. She hadn't wanted to see the ugly chair she had fucked him on, the shag rug she lay with him on while they watched a movie. She dropped the box on the counter, suddenly angry.

"Why the fuck didn't you call me, Shawn?"

"Because you asked me not to."

"I know what I asked you, but—"

"But what? Was I not supposed to believe you?"

"Well, yes, but if you cared at all, I thought you might have at least called to check and see if I was okay."

"Why wouldn't you be? You told me it was what you wanted."

"It was." She hung her head. She was embarrassed now.

Shawn shrugged. "Well?"

Lynn threw her hands up and the words came spilling from her lips. "See the thing is, Shawn, at one point, I really thought we could make this work. Like that weekend we went down to the beach for my cousin's wedding. I was excited about that. But then we were sitting there and it was this beautiful scene. And she came walking down the aisle, just the loveliest thing you ever want to see all dressed in white and I watched her drift toward her fiancé who was standing there waiting with tears in her eyes and I thought to myself, 'I want that, too,' and suddenly I wanted to tell you that. But I looked over at you, Shawn, and you were sitting there with your hands in your lap, your eyes closed. You were sleeping. You were bored, disinterested. That's when I knew."

"Knew what?" Shawn folded his arms across his chest.

"I knew that was all there would ever be with us."

"Well there you go. I guess you did what you had to do then." Shawn began sifting through the box. "Is this everything?"

Lynn nodded. "Except I was thinking that maybe . . . oh never mind." There. That was what happened every time she was near him. Everything changed and suddenly she didn't know her ass from a hole in the wall.

"Look, I'm just gonna go now," she managed before turning and reaching for the doorknob.

Shawn cocked his head and twisted his lips. He reached into the box and pulled out a CD. He pushed it toward her. "This is yours."

"I don't want it. You keep it. Listen, Shawn, just keep everything in there, okay?"

"Even this?" He held up the box of saltwater taffy. "You love these, don't you?"

"No, I don't. I never did. And if you ever paid any attention, you would know that. Besides, I don't have much of a sweet tooth these days."

"Well, you did once. You had one hell of a sweet tooth if I remember correctly." Shawn got closer, close enough to touch her if he just reached out.

Lynn backed away. "Things change. Everything that feels good isn't necessarily good for you."

She repeated in her mind the mantra she had taught herself on the way over.

Don't let him touch you. If he touches you, then it's over. If he touches you, you'll be right back where you started, your head in the clouds, him clinging to your skin like mist. You get out of here without him touching you, without him getting so close that his scent seeps into your pores, and you'll be just fine.

Shawn opened the box and pulled out a piece of the wax wrapped taffy. He popped it into his mouth. He held a piece out to her. "Sure you don't want one?"

"No thanks," Lynn said, turning toward the door. "Now, goodbye, Shawn."

Shawn shrugged, his mouth moving slowly, chewing the taffy. "Bye, Lynn."

He reached for the doorknowb and before she knew it, he had done it, had touched her shoulder. It was just for a second. It was just a little squeeze that meant nothing and everything all at once and suddenly she could no longer feel her legs beneath her. The door frame caught her before she crumpled into a pathetic mess at his door, and she leaned against it a moment, fighting for breath, fighting for the will to walk away.

But there was his hand reaching out to her and she took it. She let him pull her to him, draw her close.

Don't let him kiss you. You let him put his lips on you and it's over. He starts kissing you and working his way down and he does that thing to you with his tongue and you're done for.

And as if Shawn heard the words, had peered inside her brain and knew just what Lynn was thinking, he brought his lips down on her slowly.

She tasted the taffy. She began licking the sweetness from her lips before it stuck. "I'm not doing this, Shawn," she said. "This is what gets me in trouble every time, exactly this."

It was true. The man could fuck the good sense right out of her. Could take off his clothes and present her with that glorious dick and she'd forget her own name. All he had to do, all he ever had to do was look at her and suddenly she couldn't speak, couldn't think, couldn't see, and her clothes, bra, panties and all would slip off and she would be looking for the softest place to fall.

That was why she should never have come inside. She knew that now. He ran his soft, full lips across her collarbone. He lingered on her neck, leaving a sticky trail across her throat.

He was kissing her and it was too late. He was kissing her and whispering in her ear and she couldn't feel her legs beneath her.

"I don't want to be any trouble, Lynn," he said, never taking his lips off her.

"But you are trouble, Shawn, you are."

Her eyes fluttered closed and she threw her head to the side, letting him kiss her shoulder.

"Let me be a little trouble then, just a little. Then you can be through with me, just like you said. If I'm no good for you, if you've got no more use for me, then you can walk out that door."

Shawn's breath warmed her neck, his fingers brushed against

her arms. He pressed his chest against her breasts. Her nipples hardened against him.

Did he feel it? Would he know that he could still do that to her with just a touch?

Lynn stepped back. But Shawn followed and his mouth was on hers. She felt the sharp edges of the taffy against her gums. It clung to the roof of her mouth, stuck to her teeth and fell onto her tongue.

They shared the sweetness. Shawn's hands fell below her waist, fumbled with the front of her shorts. In one quick motion they were undone and hanging loosely from her hips.

Shawn pressed deeper onto her lips, pushing the taffy into her mouth with his tongue. He moved it around inside, lacing her mouth with the bitter sweetness. Then he swept it back into his own.

Shawn planted sticky sweet kisses on Lynn's dark skin. He reached for her and brought her to him. His skin stuck to hers, clung to hers like glue. Shawn reached around and slipped off her bra. He fumbled with her panties, pushed them over her hips and down her thighs. They gathered around her ankles. Lynn stepped out of them and kicked them aside.

Shawn leaned down and took one of her breasts into his mouth. The taffy had gone soft. Lynn felt it rub across her nipple, leaving its sticky sweet remnants.

His hand fell between her legs, pushing her thighs apart and rubbing her cunt until she was wet. And then his fingers were inside her. Lynn was suddenly thankful for the wall behind her, for the support when she felt her knees would weaken and she would slide to the floor. She reached down and touched him, wondering at what point he had become hard.

He stepped closer. She felt him rubbing against her, his dick teasing her cunt.

And then, like she knew she would, Lynn began to beg for it, was grabbing Shawn by the wrists to bring him closer and whisper in his ear.

"Please," she said, returning the sweet kisses against his ear. "Please, Shawn."

Shawn spoke between kisses, between touches, between strokes. "Do you want to be through with me? Do you want me to stop?"

"Fuck that. Fuck everything I said." Lynn was breathless. Her mouth was dry.

Shawn held her arms high about her head, his hand holding her wrists. She sucked the sweetness from his tongue, from his lips. He then slipped his pussy-tinged finger inside her mouth, allowing her to taste herself. He slid in the remainder of the taffy, letting the taste of the soft, sweet candy mingle with the taste of her cunt.

Shawn reached for another piece of taffy before he kneeled in front of her. He opened it and held it between his teeth. He leaned forward and rubbed it over her clit, pushed it in and out of her pussy with his mouth. Then he devoured her.

He pressed his mouth onto her cunt, his tongue darting in and out of her. She felt the taffy, she felt his tongue. Lynn reached down and gripped his head with her hands, pushing his mouth hard against her.

"Tell me again why we can't do this anymore?" he asked, his tongue flicking against her clit.

Lynn felt as though her knees would give in. She trembled against the feel of Shawn's tongue inside her.

She arched her back. "I don't know. I don't . . . I'm not . . . I'm not getting any younger, Shawn." Her breath came heavy. "And how many orgasms can one have in a lifetime, really? Because after all the sex is gone, what do we have left? Do you even know me? Do you know what I like?" She folded her lips, bit down on them hard.

"I think I do."

Shawn lifted her leg, threw it over his shoulder. Lynn pushed her calf against his neck, pulling him close. His tongue plunged into her, exploring the insides of her like a hunter searching for his prey.

His hands gripped her ass and held her close to his face. He moved the taffy in and around until it was gone and Lynn came in vicious shudders against his mouth. Shawn rested his head there, his cheek warm against her thigh. His breath came in hard pants.

He stood up and kissed her neck, her chin, and finally, her mouth. She tasted the saltwater taffy, she tasted Shawn, she tasted herself. She tasted remnants of herself. She savored the sweetness that lingered on his lips, bitter, sweet, then gone.

At a quarter past one Lynn jolted out of a peaceful sleep. She looked over at Shawn tucked comfortably beneath the covers. She reached beneath the sheets and stroked his belly, watched the calm that spread across his face. She relaxed against the pillow and nestled her chin against his neck and flicked her tongue against his ear.

She would have to leave him and she knew it. She exhaled. He reached over and rubbed between her thighs. She squirmed beneath the covers, her lips curving into a smile.

Only, it would have to wait until tomorrow or maybe next week. Yes, she'd leave Shawn next month for sure.

Banana Afternoon
by Jolene Hui

I was flipping through my recipe box when I found it—the perfect recipe. My mother's banana cake recipe was my favorite recipe of all time. I used to make this cake at least twice a year—carefully mashing the bananas in a dish, the scent filling my nostrils. The smell reminded me of summer and winter all wrapped into one. I could almost picture myself prancing around in my mom's kitchen in my old red bikini with the smell of banana cake in my nostrils. Making this cake was the only real time I ever could relax in the kitchen. And I hadn't done it in so long.

The day I rediscovered the recipe I was wandering around without a bra because of the hot summer weather. I needed to wear next to nothing to survive in the 105-degree heat. It was a Sunday, a per-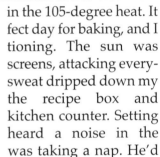fect day for baking, and I didn't have air condi-tioning. The sun was seeping through my screens, attacking every-thing in its path. The sweat dripped down my forehead as I closed the recipe box and walked over to the kitchen counter. Setting the card down, I heard a noise in the other room. Marcus was taking a nap. He'd had a long night. As a musician, he often had gigs that lasted until the early morning. It was noon when I began to cook. I could hear him rustling the covers.

I climbed up onto the counter to sort through my cake pans. I wasn't sure what one I wanted exactly. I had inherited a variety of pans from my mother. I tried to be quiet as I clanked through all the pans, but I knew I was making too much noise. Marcus would awaken at any second and wonder what was going on.

As the oven preheated, I started to sweat even more and the curls from my long black ponytail stuck to my moist neck. I had always cleaned the house naked and the heat was so unbearable it was time to experiment with nude cooking. I stripped off my white tank top and little cotton shorts and was left with my favorite panties, white lace with little black bows along the top border.

My theory that I was being too loud was confirmed as I heard Marcus awaken and slam the bathroom door while I was humming and mixing in the baking powder. I sipped my iced tea and continued my mixing. My entire kitchen felt like the center of the sun as the oven heated up, anxiously awaiting the cake to be inserted into its hot center.

"What are you doing in there?" Five minutes after entering the bathroom, Marcus stepped out of the bathroom clad in a fluffy green bath towel. His semi-long blonde hair dripped onto the floor.

"Baking, why?" I bent over, ass up in the air and picked up a piece of banana that had fallen to the floor.

"Ahhh," Marcus said, still standing in the same spot. "Can I watch you?"

I sucked the banana off my finger as I stared at his damp face, "Yeah, sure, why not?"

The cake batter smelled good as I finished mixing it. "Shit, I forgot to flour the pan!"

Marcus was now sitting in his towel on a barstool in the doorway of the kitchen. "Why don't you just make cupcakes?" he asked and shrugged his shoulders.

"You're a genius," I said as I climbed back onto the counter to dig through my pans once again. I could smell Marcus sitting on the stool. He had just shaved and his aftershave was floating around the kitchen, up my nostrils and into my little bowed undies. The flour I had carelessly spilled on the countertop stuck to my shins as I dug through the pans. The sweat had made my body sticky and the flour was clinging and hardening onto my damp legs.

"Eureka!" I yelled as I found my two cupcake tins. I couldn't even remember the last time I'd used them.

Lining the tins with multi-colored paper cups, I asked Marcus about his gig. "So, did you have groupies all over you last night?"

"Of course," he answered. "Would you expect anything less?"

"Oh shut the hell up," I said, finishing up with a blue paper cup.

"No, there weren't many groupies there," he said, "and I only thought about your sweet ass all night." Marcus ran his fingers through his hair and wiped his hand on his towel.

"Why don't you take your towel off?" I asked him as I spooned the batter into the cups.

"Just because you're naked doesn't mean I wanna strip down completely," he said, smiling. His eyes lit up as he stood and folded his arms across his chest.

My eyes shifted down as his towel loosened and fell to the floor.

"Join the club," I said as I sucked the batter off of my fingertips, one by one.

I finished filling the paper cups and put the pans into the steaming oven. They had to cook for 20 minutes—no more, no less. I carefully adjusted the timer. I would be devastated if my cupcakes didn't turn out perfectly. When I started to clean the counter, I heard Marcus approaching. He put his arms around my waist as I wiped down the bits of flour, sugar, and banana from the tile. I turned the water on and filled the mixing bowl as Marcus ran his fingers up and down my sides, tingles of pleasure ripping through my body. I grabbed the sponge and started to rinse all the spoons as his fingertips grazed my bare back and went down to the white lace panties I loved so much. My back arched and I moaned as he grabbed my ass and began to lick the sweat off my neck.

"Mmmm," I said softly. "I'm trying to clean up."

"So am I," he said as he hooked his fingers into my panties and slid them down to the floor.

I moaned and switched the water off. I felt his warmth on me as his fingers found their way to the front of my body. The scent of his clean hair and aftershave filled my pores as he stroked my wet center. I turned around and faced him quickly, my lips meshing against his, the batter on my lips rubbing all over his freshly shaved face. His hands moved quickly to my hips and he placed me on the freshly wiped countertop. I ran my fingers through his hair—the smell of baking banana cupcakes heavy in the thick air. I had accidentally decorated my chest with batter as I was spooning it into the pans, but Marcus quickly helped clean me off with his hot and able tongue. I spread my legs as I felt his throbbing cock getting closer and closer to me. I shrieked with delight as he finally shoved it in and my body slightly slipped toward him on the moist countertop. I breathed in soft quick breaths as he cleaned the batter off my body and expertly slid in and out.

When it started to get too slippery, he pulled out of me and helped me off the counter. He turned me around and began to kiss my back while pushing me slowly to the ground, my back still to him. After adjusting my body, he found me once again, sliding in and out of me while my hands were immersed in the cupcake ingredients on the floor. He leaned over me and I felt his hair grazing my shoulders. His tongue on my ear, I screamed with pleasure as the ripples burst through my body.

We collapsed to the floor as the buzzer went off on the oven. Still breathing heavily, I left Marcus on the floor and stood up suddenly. I didn't want my cupcakes to burn. Grabbing my two favorite plaid oven mitts, I removed the freshly baked cakes from the oven and placed them on top of my stove.

Marcus was still on the floor when I took off my oven mitts and went to the pantry to retrieve the items for the frosting.

"You never give up, do you?" he asked, sitting up, his right arm covered in flour.

"I have to start making the frosting," I said, feeling his come running along my right leg. I reached down, wiped it off with my index finger and sucked it off as he stared at me with satiated eyes. I broke the staring contest with Marcus and gazed into the pantry, taking inventory of what I needed.

"These cupcakes better be damn good," said Marcus, lying back down on the floor, not caring that he was slathered in all of the cupcake ingredients.

"Of course they are," I answered, offended. "I wouldn't be making them if they were gross."

I grabbed a clean mixing bowl from the bottom shelf and began adding ingredients. It was a simple frosting, with powdered sugar, melted butter, and vanilla. Marcus yelled at me from the floor, "I think you should come back down here."

I ignored him as I vigorously whipped the frosting.

"Ally, I think you should come back down here."

I felt the sweat starting to form again on my forehead and my upper body. I knew this recipe by heart and decided to make a little extra as a surprise for Marcus, who was still on the floor, begging me to come back. The cupcakes would take quite some time to cool off so I took two full handfuls of frosting and turned toward Marcus.

"What are you going to do with those?" He asked, a huge smile creeping across his face.

"What do you think I'm going to do with this?" I questioned him back as I walked to him, hands still full of the frosting. "You know this is pretty much just sugar, right?"

"I know what it is," Marcus put his hands behind his head and stretched his legs out.

I knelt down to him and put one handful of frosting on his stomach. He shrieked at the stickiness of it. "What are you going to do with that other handful?"

"Give me your hand and you decide what you want to do with it," I responded.

He stuck out his hand and I gave him a chunk of the sugary frosting.

"My turn first," I said as I started rubbing the frosting all over his body. My tongue began to lick it all off and I could feel Marcus twitching with pleasure. I licked his stomach and his shoulders, my saliva leaving trails on his skin. I worked my way down to his lower stomach and when I got to his cock, it was already throbbing and hard. I placed my mouth around it and thoroughly cleaned it off, sucking and licking as necessary. When I was finished, Marcus rubbed his frosting on the floor, rolled on top of me and entered me with lightning speed. He stuck his tongue in my mouth, tasting all the frosting I'd just licked off his body. I moaned as he plunged harder and faster, running his frosting laced fingers through my hair and tugging on it as he came closer to coming. I was aware of the pile of frosting on the ground and took it in my left hand, slathering it the best that I could across my chest. I pushed away from him, rolled him over onto his back, and got on top of him, my frosted tits in his face. He graciously sucked and licked them as I moved my hips up and down on his. With an iced thumb, Marcus rubbed my clit and I groaned with pleasure, exploding all over him, lost as he moaned and came inside me.

As we reclined on the floor and stared at the ceiling, we were aware that Marcus would need to take another shower and that I definitely needed to frost the cupcakes before the frosting dried out. Slowly standing up, I made my way to the countertop and gave the frosting a quick stir before I carefully frosted all of the 24 perfect banana cupcakes. I handed one to Marcus who had also stood up by that time. We looked at each other and laughed at each other's iced body hair and when I finally bit into the cupcake, I was so overcome with joy I didn't mind that the leftover chunks of icing on my body began to melt. That cupcake was the most heavenly thing I'd tasted all day. Well, almost.

Sugar Mama
by Rachel Kramer Bussel

"Food is love" goes a popular saying, and no one knows that better than me, though I might change it to "food is love, and sex, and friendship, and seduction." I can't seem to ever visit anyone or have a date without wanting to feed my lover, and the sweeter the offering, the better. It's not just the Jewish mother in me that gets off on serving up delectable goodies along with my voluminous breasts and eager-to-please mouth. It's more that I want my lovers to be fully satisfied, I want to fill them up in every way I know how. I want to make them scream and moan and smile and purr, want to offer them my body to suckle and taste, but when they're done with me, I want to give them something more—something sweet, something they can savor, that will stay on their tongues after our kisses end and remind them of the good times we've had. I'm like that even with friends, but with lovers, I become a sugar mama par excellence.

Take my latest boyfriend, Todd. We met at a wine tasting, where we soon found ourselves bored with all the pretentious posers around us, and headed off to a greasy diner to enjoy beers and burgers. We each savored our meals, eating slowly so as to maximize the pleasure we got from each bite, and I found myself getting turned on watching him dip each french fry slowly, almost sensually, into the pile of ketchup he'd poured onto his plate. But my panties really got soaked when the waiter came around and asked what we wanted for dessert. I was content with a cup of tea, was even considering splurging on a hot chocolate, when Todd announced that we'd be sharing the banana split, then grinned at me as the waiter walked away. I was about to protest, to claim fullness or a diet, but the way he was looking at me, so expectantly, so eagerly, so, well, *hungrily,* made him hard to resist. He looked like he wanted to devour me—right after he got done with the dessert. And let me tell you, that man knows how to savor a banana split. It came with two spoons, but we decided to only use one, and he made sure to share, scooping up one spoonful of whipped cream sprinkled with nuts and chocolate sauce and offering it to me, then holding onto the spoon as I sucked the sweet treat off of it, before taking another for himself. Eating the gargantuan dessert was our form of foreplay, complete with moans, our feet joining under the table as we gorged ourselves. When he leaned over to kiss me across the table after the last bite had been eaten, our mouths cold and sweet, I was a goner. We went back to his place and quickly pounced on each other.

That first moment I climbed on top of him, got to run my fingers through the hair on his chest, got to watch myself rise up and down along his hard dick, I was smitten. I came so fast and hard my head hurt, and I had to get up and turn out the light. We fell asleep all piled together, and when we woke up at two in the morning, his cock was hard again. I slithered down to the ground and took him in my mouth, giving him a slow, sensual nighttime blowjob, then swallowed every drop of his come. Somehow, though, when he dozed off to sleep, I was still wired. After kissing his forehead, I covered him with a blanket and poked around his kitchen. It was a typical bachelor pad, though he did show a fondness for salad dressing and had a vast array of breakfast cereals. The cupboards proved slightly more useful, but I found that I wasn't really hungry, but wanted something sweet, something I could offer him when he woke up, something I could take between my fingers and hold up to his open lips. The freezer proved a bonanza with an unopened roll of chocolate chip cookie dough, the kind that always seems so seductive in the grocery store, all squishy and sugary and salty, able to be eaten raw or warmed to just the right soft, crumbly consistency in the oven. I'd been standing there naked, letting the icy air blast my skin as my mouth watered.

I took out a cookie sheet, feeling every inch the naughty homemaker, and greased it with a stick of butter. Then I opened the roll, not resisting the impulse to sneak a finger inside the gooey concoction and grab a small nibble for myself. I managed to get a chocolate chip, and I savored it against the backdrop of the dough. Then I cut them into approximately even sizes, spreading them around the tray before popping it into the oven. I tidied up his kitchen, running a fresh sponge along the counter, even opening the fridge to swab its insides. I saved some cookie dough for later, and watched as the small circles spread inside the oven, oozing outward into perfectly warm, soft, pillowy delights. He woke up just in time for the first batch, his hair mussed, looking groggy but intrigued.

"What are you doing in here? Come back to bed," he demanded.

"Soon. You go back to bed and I'll be there in a few minutes," I said soothingly, noting his erection nesting against his boxers.

I did return not ten minutes later, bearing a tray full of cookies, their aroma wafting in the air. I hadn't used the whole roll, so there was still some dough left in the freezer. As soon as he saw me approaching with the tray, Todd did a double take, then started to laugh. "What are you doing, you crazy girl?"

I just smiled and said, "I'm bringing you breakfast in bed—a breakfast of sex and cookies, that is." But when he reached forward for one, I shook my head. "Oh, no you don't. I'm going to feed these cookies I just baked to you at my own pace. Put your hands down, or I'll have to tie them behind your back."

My words came out harsher than I'd intended them, but they had their effect. True to my sexy sugar mama roots, I wanted to feed my lovers, but I was also a control freak, so I wanted to do it my way. "Now close your eyes," I said gently, pulling a little bait and switch as I cooed into his ear, letting my tongue dawdle along his tender earlobe. I kissed and licked my way down his neck before easing my way back to his lips, holding the tray behind me with a mitt. When he started to squirm in earnest, I stopped. "Now, open your mouth, but keep your eyes shut," I instructed. When he did, I slipped him a tiny morsel of cookie, filled with an oozing chocolate chip.

I kept on feeding him from my fingertips, gooey mounds of salt and sugar and chocolate that made him moan and his cock spring up—my mouth watered at the sight. I eventually let him open his eyes so he could see what was going on. I kept on taking little nibbles myself, watching his eyes bulge as I sensually danced around him, trailing a warm cookie along my skin, letting it surf over the curve of my breast, down along my gently curved belly, along my leg, then gliding gently past my pussy. I bent over, offering him my ass, with a cookie on top. I took one of the warm concoctions and crumpled it in my hand, smushing the crumbling remains into his eager mouth, letting him lap at me until every last trace was gone. I gorged him on cookies, shoving them in way past the point of fullness, until he held up his hand and moaned, "Enough, enough! I want something else."

He grabbed me, tickling me into submission until I put the almost-empty tray on the floor, the few burnt cookies looking forlorn as they were left behind in favor of other, tangier, delights. I clambered on top of him, shoving my hands against the wall as he ate me with way more gusto than he'd shown to even that first fresh-from-the-oven cookie. His tongue, in a word, devoured me, his wide mouth seemingly everywhere at once, diving deep inside and finding every last sweet droplet of goodness, not missing a single crumb. He ate me like I was his last meal, and I pressed myself down against him until I crystallized and shattered, shaking, my hands trembling against the wall as he gorged himself on the tastiest treat around—me.

The next time he called, after our little cookie dough orgy, I felt weird walking in empty-handed. It just didn't seem like enough to not have a treat, aside from myself, to pop into his mouth. Even though I made sure to wear my sexiest lingerie, including my laciest bra, the one that presented my nipples through its fabric so he'd instantly want to start sucking, I wanted something else to feed him. I settled on roasting marshmallows as a cheap and easy way to satisfy our needs. Plus, there was just something so soft, and sexual, about them. Squeezable, like my breasts, where I surreptitiously stuffed them between my cleavage, letting the sugared coating wear off on my skin. Maybe I wouldn't even need to roast them, I thought, as I squeezed the bag while driving home, copping a feel as the gelatinous dessert morphed in my hand.

I decided to forgo propriety and stuff my bra full of marshmallows, padding it until it practically overflowed. It would need extra dry cleaning, if it could even be laundered, but it was worth it. We went out to dinner, where I let him ogle my newly sprouted breasts until he just couldn't stand it anymore. "Carla, I just have to ask . . . did you do something to your breasts? They look bigger. I can't stop staring at them," he said, a glazed look coming over his boyish face. I suddenly knew what I would do with the mushy white puffs, which felt like they were melting against my breasts.

"That's for me to know and you to find out," I said primly, lifting my napkin and daintily wiping my glossy lips, then putting it down and picking up my fork, delicately sliding it into a pile of rice and lifting a tender mouthful to my lips. He put his utensils down and slipped his foot against mine as I finished. When the waiter came around, he hurriedly asked for the check, then offered the man his credit card before he could walk away. Clearly, someone hadn't had their RDA of sweets yet.

I drove home, pushing his advances away, watching out of the corner of my eye as his dick rose against his pants. I relished my secret surprise, my sex tingling at the thought of Todd licking off every last bit of sugar from my skin. When we got inside, just for fun, I ordered him to crawl up the stairs, just to see if he'd do it. He did, and I admired his ass as I climbed behind him. "Lie down and take off your clothes," I instructed, slipping off my shoes as I spoke. He undressed, and I got a shiver as he unveiled his cock, swollen and stiff, meaty and hard. I wanted to slide it into my marshmallow love tunnel, coat him with a dusting of fine white powder, lick off every last drop, but instead, I ordered him to shut his eyes, then shucked off my dress. I moved his hands up above his head, lightly rubbing against his cock.

He moaned, and I settled my chest above his face. "Come to mama," I coaxed, pushing his face between my breasts. I'd managed to cram a lot of marshmallows into my bra, but Todd was even more voracious than I'd given him credit for, as he gobbled each one, moaning as the soft white puffs glided into his mouth. When he applied his ravenous tongue to my nipples, I was in heaven. My breasts were sticky, and there were still a few marshmallows stuck to my sweaty skin, but he ignored those in favor of more delicious delights. He sucked and sucked on my buds, tugging and toying with them before finally giving me what I most wanted—his teeth. I looked down to see the rapture on his face, his eyes closed, mouth moving rapidly as I pushed as much of my hanging boobs between his lips as I could.

The more he massaged my nipples, the deeper the ache in my cunt until I simply had to stroke myself, then shove two fingers inside me while he kept right on going. He'd pause to lick the tunnel between my breasts while they brushed against his cheek, occasionally taking a stray marshmallow into his mouth. He opened his eyes with one between his teeth and then practically gave it a blowjob, savoring every last bite, his shiny white teeth gleaming against the dessert he was devouring. I just couldn't help it—I pinched his cheeks, finally dropping my breasts down toward his chest so I could kiss him. Then I took his long, slender fingers into my mouth for a tongue bathing. With each brush of my tongue against his sensitive digits, he moaned. I finally pulled his glistening fingers out from my lips and guided them down below, where three immediately slipped inside, finally filling me. I reached down for his cock, taking it out and slowly stroking him until he erupted.

Then he didn't ask or tell, he just showed me what he wanted, pushing me onto my back and bringing his face to my sex, eating me in the most spectacular way I'd ever experienced. All I can really tell you is that I saw stars behind my closed eyes, felt his hot, greedy tongue all over me, then fingers, then everything all at once. I whimpered, then felt tears brush against my eyes as he kept right on going, this time, taking what his sugar mama had given him and then some. Todd didn't stop until I was well past four orgasms, and even then, I felt the impression of his tongue on my overheated sex. He ended things by licking one long, beautiful line from my clit on up, catching the salt of my sweat and the leftover sugar, bringing them both to my mouth.

Our most recent date involved a midnight movie—to be honest, I forget exactly what it was, because I spent most of the film otherwise occupied. While he went to the bathroom, I raided the concession stand, buying my favorite candy, peppermint patties. I slipped one into my mouth, letting the small round treat suffuse my taste buds with its spicy sweetness. His eyes were on the screen, riveted by threats and explosions, so he didn't notice as the chocolate and peppermint disc silently caressed my tongue, making nice until it seeped all along my taste buds. He certainly noticed, though, when I sank to my knees, quietly unzipped him, and gave him a quick, dirty, and tingling blowjob. He couldn't speak, which I knew he'd find maddening—most of our cocksucking sessions are filled with the filthiest talk imaginable, and hearing him tell me to swallow him whole as he tugs on my hair always sets me off. Instead, he just looked at the screen, not wanting to give anything away. The taste of peppermint was fading into the taste of cock, the heavy male muskiness suffusing my senses until he spurted a fat load against my tongue. Quick as a flash, I swallowed, zipped him up, got back in my seat and fished out the bag of candy. I palmed one and offered it to him. He didn't look at me as he unwrapped it, but as the circle hit his tongue, I saw his body jerk in his seat, and smiled to myself as I opened my final patty, a well-earned reward for my efforts.

What he didn't know is that I also had some red hots tucked away in my bag—but I'd save those for next time. A good sugar mama's gotta be prepared, and I plan to stock my purse, and my pantry, very well. They'll be my own private candy stores, ones that only open for one very special customer.

Green Chile Chocolate
by Bianca James

I met the Chile man when I was nineteen, traveling with my husband on business in Albuquerque. We had been married only two months then. It was a marriage that had been frowned upon by everyone but my money-hungry parents. David Miller was an aging industrialist bachelor who had fallen for me after I'd won the Miss Virginia beauty pageant. My beauty was all I had my entire life. My family was poor and I had been raised in a trailer, pouring all my hopes into pageant dreams. When David proposed, I didn't know him very well, or even love him, but I knew the opportunity for wealth and a comfortable life for my parents might not come twice, so I accepted. I lost my virginity to him on a week-long honeymoon in Puerto Vallerta, and then it was back to business for him, and the life of a rich housewife for me.

David was busy in meetings all week long, so I rented a sports car and went driving around the sprawling urban landscape under the shade of the pink Sandia mountains, dressed in a long green silk dress, fur coat and high heels. It was the middle of November, right before the real cold hit. I passed the long hours getting my nails done, watching movies, and shopping for jewelry and folk art knick-knacks for my family. It was an idle life, but having all the money I could spend was still a novelty then.

Triumphant at having scored a bargain on a particularly flashy piece of silver and turquoise jewelry in Old Town, I passed by a sweets shop that advertised chocolates flavored with green chile. I had been told by many natives that "red or green?" was the official state question—red or green chile, that is. It seemed like a pointless question to me, since the answer was invariably "green." It seemed that everywhere we went served green chile: drowning in soup, stuffed in burritos, slathered on every food imaginable. I didn't see what the fuss was all about: they didn't even have the spicy kick of red peppers. I didn't understand the local obsession.

However, I did like chocolate. It was something I'd always denied myself when I was a beauty queen. Now that I was married and out of the pageant circuit, it couldn't hurt just to have a little piece. David wouldn't approve, but he wouldn't have to know. And the idea of green chile chocolate was just strange enough to pique my curiosity.

I walked into the store, and was hit was a blast of warm, sweet air. I let the heavy coat slide off my shoulders to savor the warmth, and breathed in the intoxicating scent of the forbidden. No one stood behind the counter, but I was faced with shiny cases filled to the brim with chocolates, caramels, brittles, fudge, and even ice cream flavored with mint, orange peel, pecan, pine-nut, and of course, the peculiar green chile essence. I wanted to devour it all.

I reached for a sample of dark chocolate pieces studded with pine nuts that rested on top of the counter, and guiltily popped one into my mouth. A smiling man emerged from the back of the store. He was about David's age, and his face had the distinct Spanish/Indian look of a New Mexico native. His skin was olive gold, the thick hair on his head as well as his moustache were lustrous black, and most strikingly, his eyes were an intense mixture of chocolate brown and clear green. I was fascinated by his handsome face, and stared for a moment before he smiled and said, "May I help you, Ma'am?"

I blushed, suddenly embarrassed to be alone with a strange man in this place full of forbidden treats.

"I was just looking," I stammered, wondering if it would look overly peculiar if I turned around and walked out of the store. I felt as if I had been caught with my hand in the proverbial cookie jar.

"Did you like the pinon chocolate?" He asked, pleasant as ever. He was on to my game.

"Yes," I said, feeling a strange sense of relief. "But what I really wanted was the green chile chocolate."

"I think I have something you'll like," he said with a smile. "Something special."

There was a small silver saucepot and a single gas burner on a table behind the counter. He turned it on and began to melt down several sizeable chunks of dark chocolate. My mouth watered as the rich, earthy odor was released from the steaming chocolate. When the chocolate was liquid, he began blending in other ingredients— cinnamon, clove, and other spices; dried, powdered chile and whole milk from a glass bottle.

"I don't make this for just anybody," he said, pouring the concoction into two heavy ceramic mugs decorated with the geometric terra-cotta and turquoise motif that seemed to adorn every surface in the city. He took a bowl of heavy whipped cream from the refrigerator and generously spooned it onto the hot surface of the steaming drinks, and handed one to me. "Be careful, it's hot."

"So what have I done to deserve the pleasure?" I asked flirtatiously, accepting the mug.

"It's been a long while since someone as beautiful as you has come into my shop," he said, without a hint of disrespect. I was used to compliments on my appearance, but his voice had the tone of a devotee before a saint. The compliment had a strange effect on my body; my nipples stiffened and the silk of my dress felt like hands all over my skin. And then I realized with some shame that I wanted him, this candy man, old enough to be my father, sturdy and muscular in his plaid shirt, heavy silver jewelry at his wrists and throat, the sort of jewelry that had the strange effect of making a rugged man appear even more virile.

I avoided his green eyes boring into my face, and sipped the chocolate instead, crying out when the heat and the spice of the peppers burned my tongue.

"I told you it was hot," he said. "Here," he said, offering me a taste of ice cream from the freezer case. "That should soothe the heat."

"You're going to make me fat," I complained, embarrassed, "feeding me all these sweets. Normally I don't touch sugar."

"You came into my shop," he said, as if he could see right through my defensive façade. "so you must have been looking for something. And besides, it looks like a few extra pounds wouldn't hurt you." The man himself had a bit of a paunch around his waistline, which did not detract from his attractiveness, but actually made him appear more solid and strong. I imagined being encircled by those muscled arms, crushed against his big chest, and felt weak at the knees. I had a husband. What was coming over me? But I knew that I had never felt this way about David's artificially white-toothed grin, his narcissistically gym-toned body in his business suits. This was a real man, I knew it.

"Why don't you let your drink cool down a bit, and I'll show you where we make the candy in the back. It's been a slow day, no one will mind if I close shop for a few minutes."

He came out from around the counter, and I felt a strange thrill when he locked the door behind me and hung the "back in 30 minutes" sign in the window. He took our mugs, and nodded at me to follow him into the back of the store.

The shop's back room was decorated with a huge shrine to the Virgen De Guadalupe, encrusted with glitter and rich with offerings of sweets, dried chiles and fresh oranges. I inclined my head to the lady as I passed, and the man led me to a row of elaborate mixing machines and long steel counters. He put down the mugs, took the fur coat from my arms, and laid it on the cold table. "Sorry there's nowhere else to sit," he said apologetically. He put his strong hands on my waist and lifted me onto the counter, which felt very high off the ground. He handed me my mug again. "Sip slowly this time," he said. "Take your time and enjoy it, there's no rush today."

I tasted the melting cream with my tongue, the way a cat drinks milk. It tasted heavenly and cool against my scorched tongue. I took a tiny, cautious sip of the chocolate, savoring the way the dark richness filled my mouth, tempered by the creamy milk and the tangy bite of the pepper and spices. It was unlike anything I had ever tasted before.

The man sat next to me on the steel counter, his legs dangling in their blue jeans and cowboy boots, a big turquoise belt buckle fastened at his waist. We sipped our hot drinks side by side in silence until he extended his hand to me and said, "My name is Victor Jaramillo. Pleased to make your acquaintance."

I considered giving a fake name for a moment, but decided against it. "Vivian Miller," I said, returning the handshake.

"My family has been running this shop for almost fifty years, using the same recipes," he boasted. For a moment I considered asking him if he had a wife and children, then decided against it—after all, I was a married woman as well.

We finished our drinks and Victor extended his hand to help me down from the counter. He didn't let go of my hand once I'd descended, but led me over to a row of well-loved steel equipment: vats for melting chocolate, pots for cooking fudge, an ice-cream maker, hooks for pulling caramel and taffy. There were trays full of prepared sweets, shelves loaded with cookbooks and utensils, and a giant walk-in freezer full of supplies.

"Do you work here all alone?" I asked.

"There are others, but I'm all alone today," Victor replied, taking a chocolate-dipped strawberry from a cooling tray and feeding it to me, as if to silence any further questions.

The dark chocolate shell cracked between my teeth and the juicy red berry burst on my tongue. I decided it was the most delicious thing I had tasted in years, even more delicious than the fancy hotel dinners David bought me. I'd always felt too nervous to eat much in front of David anyway. I decided I wanted another, and I brazenly snatched a green stem from a neighboring tray, and popped the whole thing in my mouth. I was shocked when my mouth exploded in fire, instead of the cool berry I had expected. My face turned red and I swallowed uncomfortably, too embarrassed to spit the thing out, though I wanted to.

Victor laughed as if I were a foolish child. "Silly girl, you should have asked if you wanted another. Those were the chocolate covered chiles. Only the brave dare to eat those!"

I looked at him helplessly, wishing he would give me something to cool the flames in my mouth. My eyes were watering.

Victor made no gesture to help me, just ran his fingers through my hair, brushing it away from my face. Before I could even realize what was happening, he kissed me with his cool lips and tongue, and I forgot all about the pain in my mouth. The area between my legs burned and tingled with obscene urgency to match the heat of the kiss. It was as if I lost control of my senses. I wanted him to push me to the cold, polished floor, tear away my dress and enter me without any explanation or apology. I wanted him to strip the pretense of silk and silver from my rags-to-riches beauty queen body and take me brutally for his own pleasure. I wanted to return the gift of liberation and desire he had given me tenfold.

It was as if the potent combination of chiles and chocolate had conspired to rob me of all inhibition. I remembered seeing a movie where they said the Aztecs would use the same mixture as an offering to the gods, or to induce a state of erotic frenzy. Perhaps Victor drugged me knowingly. I did not care.

When Victor pulled away from the kiss, I buried my cheek against his shoulder and took his hand. I guided it under the silk of my skirt, along the silk of my thighs, up into the wet crevice between my legs, where his fingers glided against the slipperiness of my sex.

I moaned as his fingers brushed my clitoris, my desire ramped up higher and harder. I was disappointed when he withdrew his fingers, slick with my juices, and looked at me with a twinkle in his green eyes as he sucked the digits in his mouth.

"Take me," I whispered, my lips brushing his ear. "Please—my body is yours. Do whatever you want." I was reduced to a hungry beggar in the presence of his masculinity.

He trailed his still-damp fingers against the hot skin of my cheek, and said, "When you walked in here today, you looked as white and pure as a lily. But now you look like a rose in bloom."

Without warning, he reached down and buried his fingers into the meat of my ass and lifted me so my arms were wrapped around his neck, my thighs gripping his waist, the wet valley of my cunt cleaved by the hard mound of his erection pressing through his jeans. He carried me back to the steel table, and laid me back on my fur coat, carefully. I tried to reach for his fly, but he pushed my hands back.

"What's the hurry?" he asked with his wicked smile. He kneeled before me and removed my shoes one by one, kissing the instep of my foot and working his way up my smooth calves and thighs, moving the flowing silk dress aside an inch at a time. When he finally reached the valley of my thighs, I was desperate, but he insisted on teasing me further, kissing me everywhere but where I wanted to be kissed. When his tongue parted the slick divide of my lips, I was in an erotic frenzy. He kissed me deep and slow there, teasing my most sensitive area with his tongue, agonizing and slow, stroking my hard nipples through my dress with one hand. It had never been like this with David. I moved my hips against him, trapped in a painfully high state of arousal with no release. My orgasm came when he slipped his finger inside me, and then two. I found release as he pumped away at my soaking cunt with his eager hand, my sex juices soaking his skin and the expensive silk and fur coat. I knew I smelled like a bitch in heat, but I didn't care.

I lay there utterly helpless, sedated by my state of intense bliss and relaxation. But I could see the fire in Victor's eyes that told me he was still pained with desire. "Forgive me," he said, unfastening his fly. "I can't wait any longer."

His cock was long, slim and brown, uncircumcised and slightly pointed, like a chile pepper. As he handled himself, I could see how painfully hard he was. I wanted to touch him, but I didn't dare. Instead, I quivered with anticipation as he positioned his penis at the entrance of my still-hot cunt. I trembled as he nudged against the seal until he thrust all the way into me, filling me to the hilt. I cried out, grabbed at his shirt and worked the buttons off with my eager fingers, so I could run my nails down his nude back, rub my breasts against his hot skin. My dress was a sweaty mess bunched around my waist. Victor pounded me so hard that I moaned in a mixture of pleasure and pain, and then he slowed down, moving so slowly inside of me that I squirmed with impatience. He knew just when to fuck me hard, and when to draw it out sweet and slow. At this point I would have traded everything—the silk, the fur, the sports car and the mansion—just to be in this man's arms forever. But I knew that he was a stranger, married with kids, no doubt, and that I could never be happy as the mistress of a candy shop employee.

"Come on me," I begged. I wanted his come all over my thighs and belly, I want to rub it into my skin and reek of sex. I wanted him to impregnate me with his child, and I wanted to raise his baby with David none of the wiser. After a few more determined pumps, he exploded on me, his come raining down on my skin.

Moments after Victor's orgasm, we were interrupted by the sound of pounding at the door. Victor raised his finger to his lips, and hurriedly began buttoning his shirt, running his fingers through his thick black hair. "Hurry up and get dressed," he whispered. "I'll be back soon." He closed the door after himself and entered the front of the store. I straightened out the crumpled dress and hid my body under the heavy fur coat. I fumbled with the compact mirror in my purse, reapplied my lipstick, then ran a comb through my hair, trying to hide the signs of passion.

After a few minutes, Victor slipped into the back room. He handed me a bag full of different kinds of candy. "How much do I owe you?" I whispered.

He shook his head in refusal, and led me to the shop's back entrance. As I stood on the threshold of the door, he grabbed me fiercely one last time and passionately kissed me goodbye.

I wondered who was waiting in the front of the shop. I was half-tempted to pass by from the street and peer inside, but I decided against it, and took the sports car downtown to find something clean to wear.

Later, in the hotel room, having changed and showered for dinner with David, he picked up the brown paper bag tossed on the bed, and pawed through it. "What's this?" he asked.

"Green chile chocolates for mom. Do you want some?"

David wrinkled his nose in disgust. "That sounds awful. Take it easy on the candy, will you? It's easier to not eat than to lose the weight later."

"Yes dear," I sighed, but in truth I'd have liked to punch him.

"Oh. Before I forget, there's going to be another week of negotiations before I can head out. You can go home early if you want to. It must be terribly boring for you all alone."

"No," I said with a mysterious smile. "I think I'd like to stay."

Rosehips Are Red
by Cheyenne Blue

"Here," you say, and put your hands on your hips, and grin as if you've single-handedly planted this entire hedgerow with wild roses.

The roses tangle amid the hawthorn, ivy, and drenched long grass. Their petals are starting to wither, turning tea-brown at the edges. They smell of the end of the English summer.

You sniff their scent. "Air freshener."

I laugh and punch your shoulder, and you grab my hands and pull me into your arms. Your head lowers and we kiss, and it's soft and wet and your tongue curls like the rose petals.

The next week we walk the fields again, our gumboots caked with mud. We skirt the field the farmer has plowed for winter wheat, duck under the barbed wire, and splash through the stream dividing the wheat from the cow pasture. Sammy, our retriever, crashes through the stream. We hear his bark, and the whir and clatter of a startled pheasant.

The low autumn sun burnishes your hair; the sunlight is weaker than the warmth in your eyes. I can see the rose hedge from a distance. The soft, pink petals are gone, trampled into the grass by the cows, but as we get closer, I can see the ripe, red pendants studding the hedge.

"Rosehips!" I exclaim, and snap one from the briar.

A thorn embeds itself in the fleshy part of my thumb, and there's a drop of blood as vivid as the fruit. You meet my eyes and lift my hand. Your lips close around my wounded thumb, lapping the blood, soothing the puncture with your warmth. I close my eyes and remember those lips on other parts of my body: on my face, on my skin, on my breasts, between my legs. I remember your tongue and its wet, hot glide.

I cup the gravid fruit in my hands and a finger caresses its round shape. "Will you still love me when I look like this?" I ask.

We return the next day to harvest the hips. We bring two plastic ice cream tubs to put them in, but we forget the gloves. The briars catch in my hair, tug on my shirt, embed themselves in my fingers. You roll up your sleeves—it's your favorite shirt, its moss green matches your eyes—and the tiny thorns scratch a pattern of weals on your forearms. They're only superficial, they can't hurt.

Green-eyed people are faery people, changelings left behind when the faeries steal a human child. Green eyes remind me of the ocean: they can be stormy and dangerous, or languid and gentle. Like you.

You bend to pick the rosehips from a low-hanging patch of briar, and your shirt comes apart from your jeans, revealing a pale strip of flesh. Fine golden hairs cover your skin. I know how you love me to brush them lightly, with barely-there fingertips. It makes you catch your breath and shiver, as if those faeries that left you behind have danced across your flesh. I move closer, bend forward and let my long hair brush over your skin like their wings.

You're startled, and jerk upright, and your shoulder connects with my chin. We both reel, rub our bruised parts, and then laugh at our clumsiness. My tub of rosehips falls to the ground unheeded as we drift together, arms finding familiar routes around each other's waists, our hips aligning subtly, until I feel the fly of your jeans pressing into my belly. I slide my hips to and fro until it's not only the fly I'm feeling.

I love that pressure as you swell against me. I love the long, hard ridge of your cock, and my answering rush of wetness. You grasp my hips, pull me closer, and kiss me. It's a deep, drowning kiss, and I melt.

"Let's go home," I say. I want to be in our bed, with your hands on my bare skin.

In answer, you drop to your knees, uncaring of the wet grass, and lower the zipper on my jeans. You press your lips into my belly, and run gentle fingers over the small bump.

"Hello little baby," you murmur. "I'm your daddy."

You move lower, taking my clothing with you, until I'm bare to the air. I spread my legs and you delve between. Your fingers map my pleasure points, and your tongue follows, lapping, tasting, long strokes across my clit, until I'm trembling on the edge of climax. One finger, then two, they curl around and press, finding the places that enhance my pleasure, that make my orgasm build unbearably until I'm shaking with the need for release. Oh, you know me so well.

I throw my head back and close my eyes, so that the sunlight forms kaleidoscopes behind my closed lids. Tiny starbursts; they're like the edge of the universe. As I get close, I sway with the strength of it. One hand finds your ear, a centering point in an exploding world. The other reaches behind me, clings tightly, and it's a tendril of rose that I clutch, and the thorns bury themselves in my hand. The hurt pushes me over the edge, and I'm strung, swaying between points of pain and pleasure.

Afterwards, you watch me, as my own fingers carry me upward into another climax.

Our kitchen is warm. Sammy lies by the range, his head propped on a chair rung. His paws twitch. He's probably dreaming of chasing rabbits.

The rosehips spill over the countertop. You're washing some of them, rattling them in a colander, removing the mud and leaves and tiny beetles. I'm working systematically at the countertop, crushing each cleaned fruit with the blade of a knife, so that the shell splits and reveals the small, white seeds. Red juice stains my fingers. My belly presses against the edge of the counter. There's enough of a bump that I can't stand as close as I normally do. All this fertility makes me horny.

The pot bubbles; the kitchen is steamy and rosy, and smells of wet dog and my cunt. I haven't washed my fingers since we returned home, and I can smell myself, blending with the sharp scent of rosehips. I slice a lemon, add it to the pot for pectin, and the juice eats into my fingertips, stinging the wounds from the thorns.

You return from the shed with a bag of apples from the orchard. Bruised, misshapen, green and brown. I chop them roughly, and throw them in the pot, peel, core, seeds and all.

"We have to strain the mix," I say, consulting a printout from the Internet. "A muslin or cheesecloth. We don't have anything like that."

You disappear upstairs, and return with a large white handkerchief. It smells of cedar and faintly of you.

"Is it clean?" I ask, and grin.

You look at me, raising an eyebrow in amusement. No doubt I'm nearly as muddy as Sammy, but I hope I don't smell as bad. Our fingers wind together in a tight clasp, and I study the dirty crescents of our nails, and the way the earth has mapped your thumbprint.

I measure the juice collected overnight from the strained rosehips and apples, and you head to the village shop for more sugar. I
can hear the car's misfiring cylinder as you putter up the lane. I take
the only bag of sugar out of the cupboard; the paper splits, and the
white crystals spill over the countertop. My fingers draw random
patterns on the blue tiles: whorls, stars, smiley faces. I lick my finger,
and the sweetness bursts on my tongue. Instantly, I crave more, and
put my face down and lap up the spilled sugar like a cat.

I smile to myself, and wonder if I cleaned the counter last night.

You return, glowing from the chilly morning, with three more
bags of sugar. I measure the correct amount, a pound of sugar to a
pint of juice, and add it to my huge old pan. The sugar grates along
the bottom as I stir. I keep stirring as I heat it, watching the cloudy
mixture turn clear. It's a muted pink, like old stained glass, like ashes
of roses.

You've left the kitchen, and I can hear you moving around upstairs, singing some seventies' pop song, loudly and not very well.
I think of you showering, shampooing your hair, soaping your chest,
the soft fur on your belly, and the pendulous parts of you that hang
between your legs. I wish I were up there with you, stroking you to
hardness, tasting your salt, guiding you between my legs until
you're so far inside me that I can't tell where you end and I begin.

The jelly wells up abruptly in the pan, and I stir frantically to
stop it boiling over. A splash lands on my hand, and I gasp, and suck
away its sweetness, lap at the instant red welt.

When you return to the kitchen with your hair in damp spikes,
I'm testing for the set. A teaspoon of jelly on a cold saucer. I push it
tentatively with a finger. When it wrinkles, says the recipe. I think
of the small wrinkle between your eyes when you're peering at the
computer screen, too lazy to get up and find your glasses. I think of
that other small wrinkle, between your legs like a seam, running up
your balls, like bunched material.

You peer over my shoulder at the jelly, frozen ripples on a pink
pond. Your finger wipes up the jelly and brings it to my lips. I suck
it in, such rosy sweetness, and then I keep sucking your warm finger. I make a little game of it, sucking your digit like a miniature
cock, up and down, running my tongue around the tip.

"Witch!" you growl and bury your face in the curve of my neck
and shoulder, nipping hard.

We bottle the jelly, together, as we do everything. We made a baby, we make jelly. Life is simple when you look at it like that. You nudge over the hot jars; I fill them using the soup ladle. Nine pink jars. The jelly is setting fast, and so we each take a teaspoon and scrape out the pan. Our fingers and mouths are sticky and sweet. Then you lift me onto the countertop, push up my skirt and move between my legs. It's the perfect height, and your cock drives into me, fast and hard. Spilled jelly is sticky underneath me, binding my ass to the tiles. When you've come, you lift one of my legs over your shoulder and smear the rosehip jelly around my pussy.

"Sweet," you murmur into my pussy. "Your mummy tastes sweet, little baby."

I run a hand over my belly, and before you sweep me away once more, I say, "If it's a girl, let's call her Rosie."

Kneading
by Shanna Germain

At work, she does not let me touch her. At work, the only things against her skin are sugar and flour, butter and water, oil and vanilla. Marzipan that sticks in the cracks of her skin. Pans and almond paste and parchment paper.

She bakes the way others perform surgery. Abrupt. Precise. Focused. As though each bun and bundt cake is a life she might save.

This morning, it is apple-cinnamon rolls and chocolate mousse cake. This morning, there is nothing but this: dust and roll of dough, apples carved into glistening half-moons, long dark fingers covered in chocolate and coffee and cream.

I stand as far away from her flying elbows as my big body and the tiny kitchen will allow. I watch and wait. In Macy's Bakery, she is Macy. And I am at her service.

Macy flips the dough over, lets it fall to the counter. Her greased fingers roll the dough into a ball. With strong fists, she punches a crater into the dough, sending flour up.

She holds out her hand to me, palm up. "Cinnamon. Two." By the flat of her palm, I know she wants sticks, not teaspoons or cups. I pull the scented sticks from the jar and place them into her hand. Macy curls her fingers around the brittle spices. The sticks snap and crackle, split and spill their spicy scent into the air. She doesn't say thank you. I don't expect her to.

The girls that Macy hires to work the counter up front, the soft sweet marzipan stick girls in their pink shirts, they giggle into their palms when they talk of us. I know what they say. I've heard them on their breaks, when they sneak through the kitchen to smoke behind the building, shivering and blowing grey air out their lungs. They say Macy is a bitch. They say the only reason I stay is because I'm fat and she lets me eat for free. Because I can't do any better.

I know they laugh to look at us: Macy's body a cinnamon stick, brown and crispy edges curled inward. Me, a blob of poorly-mixed dough, pasty and lumpy and rising in the heat.

Macy drops the cinnamon crumbles into the dough crater, then plunges her hands into the mixture. Leans her body forward, press and roll, press and roll. Her forearms are wiry, criss-crossed with pale pink scars. She's always reaching into the oven to grab something at the perfect moment. "The perfect moment doesn't wait for you to find an oven mitt." This is something she's taught me.

Macy exhales, lifting her chin, careful to blow her breath away from the dough. Then she leans her ear toward me. "Hair," she says. I am ready. I grasp the stray curl between my fingers. It is wiry and flour-coated. I tuck the strand back behind her ear, careful not to touch her cheek or the little cinnamon bun swirl of her earlobe.

When she starts pulling small chunks of dough off with her fingers, I grab a pan from beneath the sink. Set it down between us on the counter. Macy rolls each little chunk of dough between her palms until it becomes a perfect globe, a little planet in her hands. Then she lays them down on the pan and I smash them against the metal with the side of my fist, my curled fingers imprinting each one with a q.

Six months ago, I started here as the dishwasher, tucking my big body behind that stainless steel machine every morning. I could crank out ten loads of battered bowls and perfectly baked-on pans and have everything put away before lunch break. Then I spent the rest of the afternoon watching Macy through the vents in the machine.

The way her head bows over the bowl, curls falling around her ears. Across her wide forehead. The way she closes her eyes sometimes, lets her long dark lashes fall down across the tops of her cheeks—the mini threads of chocolate she sometimes uses as cake icicles. The way she sometimes leans into the dough as though it is a sleeping child and she is listening to its breath. My hands pretend to scrub a pot, make circles with the sponge, but my eyes are on Macy.

I started working at the bakery because I thought I wanted to learn how to bake. That I wanted to be able to whip together all the things I love to eat: éclairs and puff pastries, cream cheese icing spread over moist carrot cake, devils food cakes and angel food cakes and those little mini-muffins with sprinkles.

But then I started watching Macy. I watched Macy bake and realized that I would never be able to cry over a cranberry crumble or swaddle rising bread dough like a baby.

And this other thing I learned too: I don't care about getting my hands on the dough or the batter or the crème brulee. The only thing I want to touch is Macy.

I watched Macy bake for three months before she called me by my name. I wasn't sure she even knew it. I was bent down sideways in the narrow kitchen, tucking clean muffin pans into their cupboard, trying not to knock into Macy's back as she mixed blackberries into brandy and sugar.

"Glory," she said. And at first, I thought it was just something she was saying, like Damn or Hallelujah. But then she said it again, Glory, and I heard her turn around and I knew she was talking to me. I stood up, looked down over the round of my belly at the tips of my black shoes. I was sure she was going to say something about how it just wasn't working out, those melted-chocolate eyes looking all the while at my pale bangs, at the constellation of freckles across my nose. Looking all the while at everything but my big body in her kitchen.

But she just reached her arm around me as though that was an easy thing. Without touching me, she pulled a drawer open near my hip. As she leaned over, I saw the curls on the back of her neck slinkied up with sweat. The loop clasp on the back of the silver necklace she always wore. And then I closed my eyes. Inhaled the baked brown sugar scent of her.

"I've got a big job today. Wedding," Macy said, near my left ear. I opened my eyes. She looked her brown eyes right at me, so close I could see the flecks of milk chocolate in all that dark. Her lips thinned and flattened until the tips of her teeth peeked out. Between the flats of her palms, layers of creamy white cloth. "I'm going to need you right here in the kitchen with me all day," she said.

I didn't know where she thought I would go. After a second, when neither of us said anything else, I figured we'd settled that. I turned sideways, tried to slide between her and the counter and the warm oven front, back to the dishwasher.

"No," Macy said. Her hands still making a sandwich of white cloths. She tapped the space on the black mat next to her with her toe. "Right here."

I waited for the marzipan girls to come, giggling at the joke. But there was only me and Macy in the kitchen. I waited for Macy to move over, to make space for me, the way people always did. But she just stood, cloth sandwich in her hands. Teeth between lips. Chocolate eyes melting me.

I put one foot up next to her toe, not touching, and shifted my weight onto the mat. My belly right up near the counter. Blackberries sweating in the red bowl of sugar and brandy. Macy's sharp elbows, her little hips and feet, so close I could feel the air swirl around them. I was afraid to inhale.

Macy's top hand grabbed a piece of cloth and pulled up. The apron opening was cake batter out of a bowl. A double recipe, falling into the pan of the floor. Macy held it out to me. "This should fit perfect," she said.

I watched my hand reach out to the apron so I didn't have to look at Macy so close. At the way her curls stuck to the back of her cheeks from sweat. At the spatters of blackberries and brandy across her own apron. At the way she was looking at me. But then I had to watch my own dough hand come near the fabric, watch my own fist shake as it grabbed the cascade of cloth.

I wanted to step back, to give myself room, but there was nowhere to go. Macy's eyes waited. I tucked my elbows in and pulled the loop of cloth over my head. The apron didn't fall over me the way it fell from Macy's hands. More like trying to ice a warm cake, the cloth catching every few feet on the way down until you felt like you just wanted to back up and start over from scratch. But finally, I was covered in cloth. Neck to knees, iced in white. I wasn't sure I could reach around to tie the strings, so I just let them hang against my legs.

I inhaled, maybe for the first time since I'd stepped up next to Macy. Summer berries and sweet alcohol inside my nose. My cloth icing didn't crack. Nothing fell. Macy didn't change her mind.

Instead, she held out her hand. In it was a silver measuring cup. "Flour, two," she said.

And so it began.

When the apple-cinnamon rolls and chocolate mousse cake are finished and placed in the bakery case, we start on the day's custom work. This afternoon, it is tiramisu three-tiered cake. This afternoon, there is nothing but this: crack and beat of eggs, lengths of ladyfingers dipped in brandy, Macy's fingers covered in cocoa and coffee and custard.

Macy is the only baker in town, maybe the only baker in the state, who will do tiramisu in tiers. For others, the soft cakes, the pudding cakes, fall always. For Macy, they rise to her will.

Macy bakes tiramisu as though she herself had just made the trip from Siena to the new world. As though she might open her mouth and pour out the flavor of frescoes and zuppas.

Instead she says, "Eggs. Eight." I hand her the big brown eggs, one at a time. She cracks each one against the side of the bowl with one hand and pours the inside over her other palm. The whites rain down into the bowl until the yolk is a cupped sun in her palm. That's when she sings. Her secret tiramisu ingredient: She sings to each step a different song. For beating the whites into peaks, it is Edith Wilson. She sings so low no one can her hear but the eggs and me. Her lips, soft and strong around notes, I can image them on my skin, tracing their sweet sugar recipes along my spine.

When she starts in like Etta Baker, those lips near-whispering "never let your deal go down" to the whipping cream, I get busy. I kiss each ladyfinger into the bowl of brandy and espresso. I layer them in the pan, one over to the other, their drunken sides just touching. "Ladyfingers like to be lined up just close enough so they don't feel alone." This is something she's taught me.

By the time the layers are finished, Macy has run through an album's, two albums' worth of songs. If there were windows in the kitchen, we could see the falling dark. Out front, the traffic has changed, become the murmur of commuters picking up their cinnamon breads and chocolate éclairs on the way home.

I start washing the dishes and Macy puts the tiramisu layers in the walk-in to chill. She takes her time getting from counter to cooler, slow-like, so the layers don't fall. They have to sit there for two hours. No opening or closing the walk-in door until then. No peeking in the walk-in window. In fact, no being in the kitchen at all unless you're Macy. Unless you're me. And even then, I better move slow or Macy's likely to squinch up her nose and send me that look, like I'm a puppy about to pee on the floor.

The marzipan girl doesn't mean to do it. I know that. Maybe Macy knows too. They're just stupid girls. So when one opens the walk-in, looking for water or her lunch or maybe just a breath of cool air, she's just doing what she does.

I hear the whish of the cooler door opening, same time as Macy. I can just see the girl's elbow around the corner. I don't know which one it is. But I know she's trembling.

"Don't close that door," Macy whispers. Even so low, her voice is knife into green apple. The girl's elbow stills. My hand around the sponge wrinkles and cramps. We wait. One second. Two. Only the low laugh of women out front, the clonk of the register drawer slung shut.

Macy takes her fingers out of the bowl of flour. Shakes them slowly. "Now, let go of the door and go back out front," she says. The girl's elbow moves out of view, comes back. Then her whole body.

"I'm sorry, Macy," she says. And then, behind her voice, a sound so quiet I can only hear it in Macy's face. They way her eyes go wide and a little wild. The way the darks rise and the rest goes white.

"Out," Macy says. The marzipan girl goes. Fast.

Macy steps softly toward the cooler. Takes hold of the metal handle. I follow, shift my weight from side to side, careful not to make a sound, careful not to move the floor beneath me. When the other two layers fall, we both hear them: Whoosh and whoosh, like tidal breaths. And then Macy too, whoosh and whoosh, the air sucked out of her.

"Glory," she says. And this time it isn't good. This time, I don't want to hear my name come out of those lips. "Glory," she says again, and then she is falling too, caving in, the final layer in all those cakes.

The marzipan girls gather in the kitchen doorway at the sound of Macy against the floor. Pink magpies, squawking and chirping. I adopt Macy's face. Eyebrows down and nose wrinkled. "Out," I say. My voice, knife into soft butter, but still they go.

Macy on the ground in front of the cooler. Her floured fingers to her face. I lower myself carefully onto the floor beside her. Macy still not moving. It's the closest I've ever been—the first time I notice the grey threads that line her curls. The first time I notice her fingernails, worn smooth from kneading, kneading, all the time. I press my finger against the back of her hand, along the L scar at the knuckle. It is hard and hot, like I imagine all of her to be.

"We'll start over," I say.

She takes her hands from her face, away from my touch. Flattens the palms against her legs. "No," she says. "I'll call and tell them we can't do it. It has to be done by tomorrow."

"We'll do it again tomorrow," I say. I press my fingertip against her floured arm. She doesn't seem to notice but she doesn't pull away either. I trace a G through the white flour and her dark hairs, G for Glory.

I watch her fingers looking for something to hold. For something to mold and build. I slide my hand palm up beneath hers. She grabs hold like my hand is an apple needing peeling.

"Let me take you home," I say.

And so we begin.

At home, I don't let her touch me. There is only this: my fingers tangled in her thin apron strings, cascade of cotton and flour against the floor, Macy's dark arms iced with sugars and spice.

My recipe is simple: Macy and me, hands and skin, kneading and heat. "The best recipes just taste complicated." This is something I plan to teach her.

Macy stands, her apron at her feet, still in her white baker's clothes, her arms at her sides.

I pull my own apron over my head, wrap the wide fabric around Macy's waist, around her hands. Still not touching. The cloth wraps her twice, three times. Macy's eyes, nutmegs in their spicy stare, watch me. The only thing on her that moves, her breath and those eyes. I lean down to tie the cloth around her. Her stomach smells of honey. I want to lick it clean.

Instead, I grab the cloth wrapping. I pull it toward me and Macy comes too, bringing her sugar scent. She thinks I might kiss her, maybe she expects me to kiss her, but I don't. I trail my fingers up her arms, the crunch of sugar beneath my skin. At first, she just stands, one foot cocked to the side like a horse, waiting. I keep my fingers there, against the skin of her arms, smoothing and pressing.

This evening, there is nothing but this: soft chocolate breasts inside my strong hands, roll and pinch of skin, my fingers lathered in Macy's dew and sweat and sweet cream. There is only her reaching, dark fingers, hungry mouth.

Inside my mouth she is the first spoonful of tapioca pudding. She is finding a fudgesicle in the freezer on a hot summer day. She is the sweet cinnamon bloom of apple pie up on the tongue. She is the perfect cake, hot from the oven.

I fuck her the way others perform surgery. Abrupt. Precise. Focused. As though each kiss is a breath of air, each slip of tongue is a sustenance and fruit.

Macy opens herself to me, lets me slip inside her. My fist enters her center, pounds her down until she rises up. Around my fingers, she lets go.

She knows I will never let her fall.

Peppermint Delight
by Michelle Houston

By nature, I'm not a nosy busy-body. But when a friend has me setting up a camera on a tripod in her bedroom while her husband is deployed out of the country, I can't help but wonder why.

"Okay, Lynette, I have to know. Why?" I gestured my hand at the camera and cocked an eyebrow at my best friend.

A deep blush colored the fair skin of her face and neck, disappearing into the collar of her shirt. "Mike's not going to be back home for our anniversary, so I'm going to take some special pictures to send to him."

I nodded. I could understand that. If my own man was stationed far away from me on our anniversary, I would send him pictures too. Although I didn't know Lynette was going as bold with them as I would have been.

"So why did I have to perform a mad dash all over the city to buy you several dozen of those damn peppermint sticks? I thought that's what you were sending to him."

"Oh, I am. Mike LOVES candy. Especially peppermint sticks. They remind him of our wedding night. Since we got married on Christmas Eve we . . . well . . . we made love under a Christmas tree for the first time as a married couple. Afterwards, we nibbled on candy canes."

I couldn't help but grin as her blush deepened. I also couldn't help but wonder what else they had done with those candy canes. Then again, maybe it was just me that would have done something else. Speaking of which . . .

"Hey Lynette, how about I take the pictures for you?"

"Oh no, Cyndi, I couldn't ask you to do that," she stammered.

"No problem. It might even be fun. Go ahead and get changed, and I'll get set up."

Oh yeah, this could be fun, I thought. I could feel my wicked juices bubbling as I imagined Mike's surprise when he opened her gift.

"Changed?" she asked.

At first, I thought I heard her wrong, but when she repeated her question, I knew she was going to start in her jeans and t-shirt and simply strip.

"Why don't you put on something naughty, maybe even a bit slutty. How about something Mike bought you, which will stir his libido, and make him wilder for when he gets home. Maybe he'll keep you in bed a week."

Lynette shook her head. "I don't have anything sexy."

I was about to suggest we run out and get an outfit, when she cocked her head to the side and mumbled, "I do have one outfit . . . but I've never been able to work up the nerve to put it on."

"Go and get it, girl. Let's see it."

Scolded puppies must have looked happier than she did as she walked to the closet. You'd think I had suggested she run down the street naked. Although, for a second . . . nah.

She handed me a bag as if it contained a poisonous snake, I couldn't help but marvel that I hadn't managed to corrupt her in the years we'd been friends. We were almost exact opposites in looks and temperament, but somehow we worked well together. Just like her and Mike. I never would have pictured such a delicate woman falling for a six and a half foot tall die-hard military man. Then again, I never guessed that same woman would become my best friend.

As I pulled the lace confection and matching stockings from the bag, I could already picture how she was going to look. Mike was going to lose it. He'd go happy though.

Before she had a chance to change her mind, I stuck it into her hands and guided her towards the bathroom. "It'll be perfect. Now, get changed."

While she headed to the bathroom, I rushed into the living room where I had left the peppermint sticks. Oh yeah, Mike was going to love his present.

I grabbed one of the sticks and rushed back into her bedroom. I just had time to unwrap it and test slide it in and out of my clenched fist before she returned. If I could just get her to go along with my plan, Mike would be forever grateful.

As I caught sight of her, I playfully whistled. Lynette blushed all the way to her navel. Which in the outfit she had on, was completely visible. Almost her whole stomach was. The stockings covered most of her legs. The rest of her torso was covered in a lace-up corset, and the barest of thongs covered her pussy. If women did it for me, she definitely would have made me creamy.

"Are you sure about this?" she asked timidly.

"Completely. Put on your red heels and kneel on the bed."

I have to admit, the sight of her ass as she bent over and strapped on her heels did cause a flutter in my pulse. I'd have to have been dead for it not to. She had the most perfect heart-shaped ass I'd ever seen.

When she stood, I moved behind her and pulled the clips from her hair. Waves of auburn tresses flowed down from her head, barely brushing against her shoulders. Running my fingers through the thick curls, I combed them out into a nice cascade that framed her face perfectly. She had taken the time to apply a light coat of makeup that accented her delicate features without overpowering her natural beauty. I found myself wishing women did do it for me.

"Let's get this show on the road." I handed her one of the peppermint sticks. "Here, you'll need this. Kind of suck on it a little."

She stuck the tip in her mouth like she would a straw. "No no, Lynette. Pretend Mike is standing right here, and it's his cock you're sucking on. Lick it a little, that's good. Yeah, just like that."

She caught on quick. I almost choked as she deep throated the striped candy, but luckily, I remembered to snap the picture.

"Swirl your tongue around the tip." I continued to coach her as I snapped pictures. "Good, hold that pose."

I could tell by her increasing bravery that she was almost ready for the next step in my plan. Her eyes had darkened, and her breath was coming in little pants. "Okay, lean back a bit and slip the right strap down, baring your breast. Good girl, now just teasingly rub the peppermint over your nipple."

Her head tossed back at the contact, even as her nipple hardened further. Hopefully, the photos would turn out as great as they looked taking them. It was good material, now that she was starting to relax.

"Part your thighs a bit and rub the candy over your crotch. Oh yeah, that's perfect." I knelt at the foot of the bed and snapped the picture. "Now, suck on it again, while you slip a hand into your panties. I want to see your knuckle tenting them out as if you're teasing your clit."

I knew my voice had grown huskier, but there wasn't much I could do about it. I was turned on by taking her pictures, and by watching her perform such intimate acts. I had always been a bit of a voyeur, but I'd never had a chance to take things this far before.

The digital camera beeped, and I glanced at the memory bars.

"Okay, take off your panties while I swap out the memory."

I turned my back to give her some privacy while I changed out the memory. When I turned back around, she was sprawled on the bed, her knees bent, and fingering herself. Maybe I had corrupted her, and she was just slow to show it.

I started snapping pictures as fast as I could as she thrust her fingers into her pussy, and pinched her nipples with her other hand. "You're doing great Lynette," I encouraged in a breathy voice. I hardly dared to speak louder for fear of breaking the spell she was under.

"Rub the peppermint over your lips again, slowly licking on it. Brush the tip of your nipples with the wet end. Just like that . . . yeah. Take the tip and slowly trail it down your stomach."

I tried my best to zoom in on the wet trail the candy left behind as she slowly slid it over her skin. "Now, part your pussy lips slowly with your other hand, and press the tip of the candy against your clit. Swirl it slowly around, rubbing your little button. Oh yes," I hissed.

The camera whirled and clicked as I snapped off a few more shots. "Slide the tip into your pussy—just enough to tease. Mike loves his candy, Lynette. Make it give him a hard-on every time he sees a peppermint stick from now on. Tease yourself with it—yeah just like that."

I wanted to slide my own hand down my pants and masturbate alongside her, but I know she wouldn't be able to handle that. Biting the inside of my mouth, I continued to take pictures.

Lynette thrust the candy into her pussy, driving a good six inches of the stick in, then pulling it out, only to thrust it back in again. I moved around the side of the bed and carefully zoomed in on her face, catching the closed eyes and the 'o' her mouth had formed as she gasped for breath. Her skin glistened with perspiration, and her corset clung to her skin with every breath. The wanton sprawl of her silk clad legs invited me to focus the camera down between them, and I know I got a few good shots of her thrusting the peppermint stick into her pussy, before she shuddered and softly screamed.

Breathing like I'd just run a marathon, I gently knelt on the bed beside her and caught a good view of the candy as it slid out of her, coated in her juices, before she thrust it back in.

Heaven above, I wanted to be fucked—right then and right there. But I reminded myself this was about Lynette, and Mike, so I kept taking pictures, even as I wanted to run across the street, throw open my dresser drawer, find my biggest vibrator, and screw it until the batteries were empty.

As she thrashed on the bed, I tried to keep my balance and take the best pictures I could. Her fingers wrapped tightly around the candy, her other hand busy playing with her clit. If Mike didn't like the photos, I was going to have him checked for a pulse. Lynette was on fire. She must have exhibitionism in her DNA.

The musky scent of her juices filled the room, mingling with the fresh scent of pine from the tiny pre-decorated tree she had on her dresser, and the sweet scent of peppermint. Christmas was shaping up to be one hot holiday.

Lynette screamed again, and slammed the candy into her pussy. I made sure to catch it on film, before shifting to her face to get one last close-up as she came.

I dropped the camera from my eyes and stood there, watching her as she slowly calmed down. Her green eyes opened and her  gaze locked on mine. For a moment, I wasn't sure what I saw there, until she whispered, "Thank you."

I nodded and turned to leave. "I'll uh, I'll have the photos printed for you by the time we head to the gym tomorrow, so come over a few minutes early and we'll sort through them."

"It's a date," she called out as I hurried from the house, stopping only long enough to grab my keys and a peppermint stick. I know I imagined it, but as I pulled the door closed behind me, I would have sworn I heard her moaning. I knew that I'd never be able to look at a peppermint stick the same way again.

The Fat Box
by Jennifer Dziura

Outside The Svelte Lady is a sign, visible from Sunset Boulevard, that says "Go Thin! Leave Life in the Fat Lane Behind!"

My picture on the wall inside hangs just above a plastic-laminated sign that reads "I lost 55 pounds!" All of the employee photos are grouped under a banner: "Everyone who works here is a success story!"

At the very end of the row of photos is a picture of Britt Redding. Instead of saying how many pounds she lost, her shiny white sign simply says "Owner."

Each session of our fourteen-week guaranteed weight loss program had a different motivational theme. Today was "Thinking Outside the Fat Box!"

Stationed at the front desk, I took money and checked membership cards as women of all sizes—aspiring actresses wanting to lose those last three pounds, obese cleaning ladies, zaftig mommy-types—strode or waddled into the back room where Britt worked her magic.

"The real you," she would say, "is hard and angular, with shapely legs, rippling abs, cheekbones. She's trapped inside your fat like a beautiful woman stuck in a mascot costume." Britt herself is kind of stringy-thin. Even her face is thin. Britt's cheekbones could cut glass, although I think she might have cheek implants, which are no longer avant-garde in L.A.

L.A., of course, is full of kinder, gentler weight loss clinics. But Britt's little diet boot camp does more business than any of them. Our front window is full of magazine articles—L.A.' s hottest new business of the millennium.

You'd be surprised how many people have to ask how to spell "Svelte" on their checks, but I knew Jade wouldn't be one of them.

She strode in looking like the L.A. incarnation of the fucking Queen of England, blonde blown-straight hair brushing the shoulders of her size 18 business suit. When I saw her, I got nervous, hunching my shoulders like I used to do before a big game.

After the weigh-in and initial pep talk, Britt sent Jade to me at the front desk to make her initial payment. "Remember," Britt said in closing, "everyone who works here is a success story!"

"You look like a success story," Jade said to me. Was she flirting? It's almost impossible to pick out a lesbian in L.A. In this town, even the dykes eat meat and get breast implants.

Jade had come just in time for "Thinking Outside the Fat Box." I pointed her towards the back room and felt bad about what she was about to hear. "Imagine," Britt would say, "in fourteen weeks, you'll finally be able to see your hipbones!"

When Jade emerged from the back room, she looked unamused, as if one eyebrow were permanently raised in a perpetual expression of "you have got to be kidding me."

Britt was already out the front door, gym bag in hand, when Jade leaned her elbow on my front desk and asked, "May I ask you how you lost fifty-five pounds?"

"The program worked for me," I said, "but everyone's body is different, and some people—"

"Did you lose fifty-five pounds thinking outside the fat box?"

Air caught in my throat. Jade leaned in closer.

"You don't look like someone who would walk into a weight loss clinic because she thinks her thighs should be thinner. You look like someone who would beat that girl up."

"I . . . played basketball in college," I said.

"So you were fat then?" she asked.

My mouth is always working faster than my brain. Crap.

"Could you slam dunk with an extra fifty-five pounds on you?"

"You're beautiful," I said to Jade.

"So when were you fat?" She said it kind of like how you'd talk to a kid whose ass you were already kicking at Candyland.

"I feel terrible." The words poured out. "It's all a lie. None of the employees here were ever fat. I was captain of the basketball team in college. I needed a job."

"I could sue, you know. That's false advertising."

I was silent. Silent and sweating.

"I thought you were staring at me because I was fat."

"No," I said. "Oh, no." I figured my job was probably already lost. I felt beads of sweat break out on my upper chest, cold little drops of sweat.

"I've been staring at you because—"

"Yes?" said Jade.

"—I wanna eat Twizzlers out of your boobs."

I didn't know I had wanted just that until I said it, but then I was just staring at the inch of cleavage visible above the "v" of her jade-colored top, and I wanted to jam-pack that hollow with red licorice and dive in head-first, with my hands on the sides of her boobs, smushing them together, spilling out the licorice into my mouth, smothering myself.

"Got any Twizzlers?"

I looked around the store. The last dieter was leaving.

I kept my candy stashed in the cubby beneath the cash register. I rifled through Junior Mints, Star- bursts, Werther's Originals, Hershey's Miniatures.

"No Twizzlers," I said. I ripped off the top of a pack of Sweet Tarts. They seemed like the most romantic candy I had. I fingered a pink one, pinched it carefully between my thumb and forefinger. Jade leaned her head in. I popped it into her mouth and she caught my finger, sucked on it, and as I pulled my finger slowly from her mouth, the wet red of her lipstick made her mouth look like the fat-test little pussy I'd ever seen.

"I can eat a lot of Sweet Tarts," she said. I fed her a purple one.

"Let me lock up," I said. I left the front desk and, as I brushed past her towards the door, she took the Sweet Tarts from my hand.

"I'll keep track of these," she said. She took an orange, two pur-ples, and a pink all at once.

I was sitting on the edge of the front desk, knees up near my el-bows, pussy facing the front windows of the store. I had closed the curtains—thank God we had curtains—but I was anxious that Britt would come back, that she would've forgotten her protein bars or Botox syringes or something.

When Jade's tongue hit my pussy I could feel the Sweet Tart sting right away. It's the same feeling you get in the roof of your mouth.

"You know I'm a compulsive eater," she said.

When I got Jade onto the couch, she finally let me dive into her boobs. Her nipples stretched enormously, like finger cymbals. I sunk my head into her cleavage. I needed to get a grasp of it all, to orient myself in this new world of swollen, maternal woman. This—oh dear God—this is why I became a lesbian, I was thinking, head buried.

Jade pulled me back out of her boobs. "Everyone does that to me," she said. "You can't crawl back in the womb, you know."

I reached under her pinstriped skirt and my hand climbed up, seeking the top of her control-top pantyhose. Soon I had two fingers inside of her, the other hand still grasping one globular breast.

Her breasts were like basketballs, the smaller ones they use in the women's game. My fingertips tightened around the left one and I imagined myself spinning it, dribbling it, shooting it skyward.

As Jade's body started to shake, I felt strong and forceful, but also lean, dried out, hard. Every part of Jade was juicy. Plump fingers, luscious round berries of earlobes, swollen-soft labia, a pussy that looked turned on all the time and even more outrageously succulent when it actually was. Her entire body looked on the verge of bursting from orgasm.

Jade didn't object when I expressed a desire to bend her over a scale. By then I had four fingers inside her, pushing upwards with all the strength in my forearms.

As I thrust into Jade, pushing up against the front wall of her pussy, I lifted her weight off the scale, and we eyed the numbers as they danced. 195 . . . 190 . . . 195 . . . 189 . . . 195 . . . 186.

I had never in my life seen anything as satisfying as the jiggle of Jade's asscheeks. I was still naked from the waist down, and I pressed my entire front pelvis into her left cheek and watched the right one undulate. Even her cellulite drove me mad. With my free hand, I grabbed the area under one asscheek. With all its dimples, it was like fractal imagery of boobs and asses, like fucking an army of big-assed, big-titted women.

I was lost in this reverie when Jade jerked forward on the scale and came everywhere, a miracle of female ejaculation made possible by the violence of a good athletic drilling.

"I'm sure I lost a pound right there," she said.

"You can't keep working here," said Jade, as we righted our-selves, and she worked back into her pantyhose. "Working here is for assholes."

"All I know how to do is play basketball," I said.

"Send me a resume," she said.

I nodded as Jade stepped back into her shoes and handed me a business card from her purse. I turned off the lights and opened the door for her. I watched that size-eighteen ass saunter out covered in pinstripe and thought, *fuck yes.* And, *fuck you, Svelte Lady.*

As I closed the door, I looked into the dark clinic, the pictures of thin people looming in from the walls, weigh station after weigh station, and I resolved to make this my last exit ever from The Svelte Lady. It smelled like sex in there. I'd leave The Svelte Lady smelling like fat chick pussy.

"Can I call you," I asked, " . . . not about a job?"

"You're not so good with subtlety, are you?"

I could still feel the Sweet Tart sting between my legs. "Um," I said, "I've been trying to think outside the fat box."

"Don't," she said.

Window Shopping
by S. Lynn Taylor

Every morning I pass Amelie's on my way to the evil place that keeps my paycheck. And every morning I stop to drool at all the decadent offerings displayed in the front window—the truffle brownies are to die for—gain ten pounds from fantasizing, and keep going. But this morning was different. I stopped as usual, Frappuccino in hand, but it wasn't the brownies that made me drool. There she was, the new pastry chef, the most beautiful confection I've ever seen. I watched as she spread out soft sugar on the counter and rolled chocolate balls in it. I wanted chocolate balls, and for her to roll them in soft sugar.

I could have stayed outside that window all day just watching, but the clock tower had other plans for me. The bells were chiming nine o'clock and I was officially late. I took off as fast as I could, running zigzag through the crowded streets, almost knocking people over. Thankfully, my office building was only one more block down. I rounded the cor-ner toward the employee en-trance, took the stairs to the fourth floor and snuck in just under the wire. The last thing I needed was to have the boss on my ass; he's about as frustrated as a man with a perpetual hard-on and the hairy palms to show for it can be. Rumor has it that he hasn't had a piece of ass since his wife left ten years ago, and they were only married two weeks.

I spent the rest of the morning trying to concentrate on the endless piles of crap that kept landing on my desk. Duplicate this, triplicate that. But all I could think about was the pastry chef and how delicious she looked in her floured apron. I mindlessly processed the forms, stacking them in four different piles depending on where they were to go next. I've been here for almost ten years doing the same boring shit, so I have no trouble multitasking. I often daydream while I work. It's the only thing that keeps me sane. My daydreams aren't always about having wild and kinky sex. Occasionally I just fantasize about having another life. One where I'm a bohemian artist living on the beach with other bohemian artists.

I imagine days spent jet setting to exotic locations snapping surreal images, and nights attending trendy gallery exhibits where my photographs are blown up giant size, a la David LaChapelle, and displayed for the art world to ogle over. I sip Godiva Chocolate Martinis and talk about the nuances of shadow and form with the likes of Annie Liebowitz, Mary McCartney Donald or Horst P. Horst. Or, I'd spend my days on the beach with my hands molding cool wet sand into some sculptural form that no other artist could conceive, and my nights molding the sculptural form of another virtuoso artist.

Great dream—except I'm about as artistic as my dog. My college art professor made sure I knew that. He actually recoiled when I turned in my final project. He bellowed, "What is this? I asked you to sketch the model posing before you, not the wicked witch from a Halloween card. You're not talented, you'll never be talented, and I seriously advise you to rethink your career choice." So I did, but I guess I can at least still dream about sipping chocolate martinis in trendy galleries.

Then, other times, I dream about having a truckload of money and my own island where I can run things exactly the way I want. Scantily clad women waiting on me hand and foot, fanning me, feeding me macaroons, and attending to my every whim and desire. Then, sometimes I do dream about normal stuff like a beautiful wife waiting on me naked at the door, ready to relieve the tensions of a hard workday. Alright, so I do almost always dream about wild and kinky sex. But today, the only thing on my mind was her.

As usual, the morning dragged, but lunchtime finally arrived. I decided to take a long stroll to try to get my mind off her. I tried to shop but the only store I went into was Pottery Barn. I found myself looking at all the kitchen gadgets and I don't even cook.

On my way back to the office I stopped for more coffee at the Starbucks next to the florist. I couldn't believe it! There she was in the shop, buying the largest bouquet of roses I've ever seen. I couldn't help it—just like this morning, I stood and stared. I've never wanted anyone so badly in my entire life; this was definitely my first experience with uncontrollable lust at first sight.

Oh shit, I thought, *here she comes.* I turned to face the street just as she walked out, hoping she wouldn't notice my stare burning a hole through her. When she crossed in front of me and smiled, I nearly melted. She continued walking and I continued following. *Great, now I've gone from voyeur to stalker,* I thought.

Time had passed so quickly that I didn't realize that I was already twenty minutes over my allotted lunch hour and thirty minutes away from the office. I knew I should head back, but instead, I pulled out my cell and dialed my boss. I lucked out with his answering machine. I left some incoherent message about girlie problems and not being able to get back this afternoon. I knew I would pay for this tomorrow with his continuous off-color comments that fell just short of sexual harassment, but I really didn't care. I just closed my phone and hurried to catch up with the pastry chef.

We must have walked four or five miles from the way my feet and calves were burning. I really had no idea where I was, or why she hadn't noticed me or what I would say if she did notice me. Part of me wanted to turn around and head back, but the part of me that was in control wouldn't let me take my eyes off her. I just continued to follow her as though she was dropping a trail of cookie crumbs.

Finally, in what seemed like another mile, she turned, going up the walkway to a small cottage that would've made Hansel and Gretel cringe. She dropped the roses in a can by the porch. I lingered back, trying not to be noticed as she disappeared into the darkened doorway. *What now?* I thought. *It's not like I could just go up and knock on the door.* "Hi, I'm your voyeuristic stalker who just followed you all the way from the florist. Can I come in and check out your lovin' oven?" I said half aloud, and then peered around nervously to make sure no one else had heard me.

I don't know what possessed me to follow her all that way. Loneliness, I guess. It'd been awhile since I'd had someone in my life, two long years to be exact. I'd never done anything like this before and I couldn't believe I had now. I was a bit panicky and decided I'd better get out of there before someone from the neighborhood watch called the police. But, as I turned to leave, I caught a glimpse of her. She was naked, her body as flawless as a freshly baked soufflé.

I stood next to a large maple at the end of her driveway, staring at her through the uncovered window. I imagined my hands kneading her doughy figure. She looked in my direction; I ducked behind the tree but could have sworn I saw her bubblegum lips smile at me again. Wishful thinking. Or was it? She seemed to move closer to the window and made no attempt to pull the shade. I tried to get out of her line of sight, but tripped over a large tree root that lay above the ground—damn heels. This time I was sure she'd seen me. She just stood there, watching me watch her.

What was she thinking? My thoughts were running wild. I could only think of my lips trailing candy kisses all over her. Starting on her forehead, then around her smoldering gingerbread eyes, onto her caramel apple cheeks and lingering on her plump luscious lips. I savored the sweetness on my tongue as I felt the candy box between my own legs start to melt, and thick rich nougat drip from my pecan cluster. My knees were getting weaker as I stood there watching her glide her own fingers lightly over her forehead, around her eyes, onto her cheeks, and then linger on her plump luscious lips as she lightly licked them.

My mind cleared for just a moment. How could she know what I was thinking? I stared at her again through the window. She had paused almost as though she was waiting on the next ingredient of the recipe. I continued to imagine my strawberry lips all over her, leading me to the finest gumdrops I've ever tasted. My hunger was uncontrollable as I envisioned licking the sugar coating off both of them. I watched again as she lifted one breast, then the other, and began to suck ravenously. Somehow I could hear her moans through the closed window; it seemed as though they rode on the air like the smell of freshly baked blueberry tarts.

My mind was everywhere now. I couldn't concentrate, not that I had been able to concentrate before. I tried hard to focus, my eyes drifting down to the most succulent offering I've ever seen. She glistened with sweet rich custard. I just knew I had to have a piece. I thought of how I would drop to my knees and take a long deep whiff; her bakery would surely be full of sinful treats.

As my mind wandered to how good she would taste, I watched as she rubbed her hands slowly down her stomach and entangled them in her bush. I finally just let my mind go. I imagined she threw her luscious mocha leg over my shoulder. Then, almost instantly, she threw her own leg up onto a chair and opened her display case wide just for me. As a kid I always went for the creamy center first and this time would be no exception. I watched as she slid her thumb in and out of her slick wet self.

In my mind, I tightly grasped one hand around her left bun, allowing my fingers to dip in and out of her special package. She followed, moving her fingers back, scratching her ass slightly and then working hard in and out of her own tightness. I couldn't take it any longer; my mind was racing. I took my free hand and pictured it grasping her éclair. I began to mold it between my fingers and thumb. Her free hand followed my lead, working her clit the same way she worked the chocolate balls earlier this morning.

I could almost feel her leg tighten around me. I braced myself against the huge maple to keep my own legs steady as I watched her stir like a mixer on high. I couldn't help myself, I moaned aloud as I closed my eyes and imagined I was there, insatiably licking the overflowing bowl. A few moments later I opened my eyes to see she had pulled the shade and to my surprise it read: Bakery Closed, Come Again Tomorrow.

Two Scoops of Gelato
by Sage Vivant

Not even my recently acquired gelato sufficiently held my attention when the storefront of La Maschera came into view as I strolled along Via Faenza that afternoon.

I thought I'd seen Italian theater masks before but one look into this shop exposed my hubris. What I'd seen in the past were third-rate imitations of the artistry now before me. My chilly cup of gelato ceased to have any importance as I looked around, awestruck.

The shop was small, as all establishments are in Florence. A narrow, hand-painted path from the front door to the artist's modest workspace was the only area unadorned by masks. *Papier mache* faces confronted me at every turn, hanging from the rafters, lurking in the corners, lounging on table tops, precariously balanced against one another. Soft, amber lights cast an occasional eerie mood upon a smiling *Commedia dell'Arte* mask or gave unexpected life to a particularly dour Sicilian one. Some of the masks were designed to be worn, but others were true works of art, fashioned for display purposes only. I felt as though I'd stepped into a museum that offered me the riches of the Uffizi with none of the cost.

A short, impish-looking man with glasses stood at the workstation, speaking Italian to someone. Although I speak very little of the language, I adore the way it sounds and noticed instantly that he spoke it with a delightful lilting cadence that matched the sparkle in his eyes. Suddenly, the reverence I felt for his art was compounded—or should I say complicated—by my curiosity about the man himself.

The visitor left a few minutes later and the artist and I finally made eye contact.

"Buona sera," he said. He wore an adorable little cap stained with paint. It sat comfortably on his head at a rakish angle that was far from studied. This was a man in his element. He emanated peace, excitement, desire, mischief, and wisdom just standing there among his creations. Meanwhile, my knees grew weaker by the moment.

"Buona sera," I replied, knowing that even that brief phrase would betray my American roots.

Nevertheless, I told him in English that his work was beautiful. I knew that even a language barrier wouldn't distort such a heartfelt sentiment.

"Grazie," he said, smiling. "What is your flavor?" He nodded toward my cup, which was now soggy with neglect.

"*Due*," I told him, showing him two fingers, sheepish about my gluttony as well as my inadequate Italian. "*Malaga e meringa.*" The woman at Vivoli Gelateria recommended the combination—grape and meringue—and she had been right. What I'd eaten of it had been heavenly. I was suddenly aware that it was a large cup and that what remained in it had long ago succumbed to the summer heat. For a variety of reasons, I thought it best not to tell him that I had sampled a new flavor every day of the twelve I'd spent in Florence. Furthermore, because I would be returning to San Francisco the next day, I feared I wouldn't be able to experience all the available flavors before my departure, so I'd been ordering two flavors a day for the past three days.

No, I wouldn't disclose any of that.

"Ah!" He said. "I love *malaga*. My fay-vo-reet. You buy at Vivoli?"

"*Si!*" I exclaimed to his knowing nod.

We laughed, and I learned his name was Gino. Normally, I go by the name of Peggy because I despise Margaret. I love the Italian pronunciation of my real name, though, so I gave him that.

"Marguerite," Gino repeated, to my delight.

To the extent that his English allowed, Gino then regaled me with the fascinating stories behind some of his masks. Seeing that my gelato cup needed attention, he offered to take it from my hand and throw it away, I presumed. I grinned when he drank the remaining gelato in one swift gulp before he tossed the cup in his hidden garbage pail. He licked his lips appreciatively and continued to tell me about Venice's Carnivale and the significance of the Pantalone mask. I liked knowing that we both had residual grape gelato on our palates.

He walked to the front window and flipped his sign from *aperto* to *chiuso*. "Oh, I'm sorry. I didn't realize you were closing," I said, truly sorry I hadn't been more mindful of the time. The sun was setting, so I guessed it had to be close to 8:00.

I don't think he understood me. "Would you like dinner? With me?" he asked.

The idea ranked as highly on my to-do list as another cup of gelato would have.

"I want to call a friend. We were supposed to meet for dinner."

"Oh, please don't cancel your plans on my account." I almost encouraged him to bring his friend along, but couldn't bear the thought of a potentially romantic evening ruined.

"Maybe he join us?" Gino asked.

Rather than blurt out "Whatever for?" I summoned my enthusiasm and agreed to the idea. Gino placed the call, conducted a conversation that continued for less than a minute, and then told me his friend would arrive shortly.

The friend must have been in the next building—he entered the shop about two minutes later, using his own key.

"Marguerite, this is Rinaldo," Gino said as I shook hands with the man in the expensive suit. Much slicker and more sophisticated than Gino, Rinaldo looked like he'd be more comfortable at a board meeting than an artist's studio. He wasn't young—probably in his forties, like Gino was—but his worldly-wise attitude made him seem like an older brother when contrasted against Gino's inner sprite.

As I followed Gino and Rinaldo one block east then one block north of La Maschera, I not only noticed that both men were shorter than I (and I am not tall), but also how each carried himself with his own unique brand of confidence. I suspected I knew the source of Gino's but was still trying to figure out what gave Rinaldo his swagger. The men seemed a very unlikely twosome to me. And I couldn't even eavesdrop on their conversation to learn more as we snaked our way down Via Panacale.

I had assumed we were heading to a restaurant of the men's choosing, but instead we ended up at the front door of Gino's house. My travel reading had warned me against going into a stranger's home in a strange land but my instincts told me that in this case, no harm awaited me. I followed the men up the winding flight of stairs inside that led to his spacious flat. The ancient walls of the building kept the air cool enough to convince me it wasn't June, after all.

Gino's masks were in evidence throughout but they never overshadowed the costumes, photos, and other art objects that populated his home. Rinaldo made himself at home on Gino's worn sofa as Gino set about putting a meal together. A pot of water was placed on the stove while he dug out some peas and artichoke hearts.

"I have idea!" Gino announced after he'd assembled his *mise en place*. "I have something for you!" His playfulness captivated me and as he scampered off to some remote part of the flat, I laughed and peeked into the living room to see what Rinaldo was doing. To my surprise, he was right behind Gino. I felt it was presumptuous to follow them, so I stayed in the small but functional kitchen.

"Marguerite! Come!" Gino called. He had to keep calling for me to find him in the enormous apartment. They waited in a room that resembled a theater's wardrobe, stuffed with racks of heavy, elaborate costumes with full skirts and intricate patterns. Gino was already wearing a gold-leaf embroidered smock that ended mid-thigh and an expressionless Sartiglia mask that could not hide the way his eyes danced behind it. He was as excited as a child playing dress-up and couldn't wait for me to don the dress he'd selected for me.

They left the room so I could struggle privately into the weighty garment. Why had Gino given me something so difficult to manage? My skin shone with a thin veil of perspiration as I fought to close the back of the dress. When it was clear I would be unable to do it alone, I opened the door to find both men waiting to assist me. Despite my backless and vulnerable situation, no liberties were taken as Gino laced up the dress, leaving me with the distinct impression that he really wanted only to cavort in the costumes, rather than use them as subterfuge for getting me naked.

Even Rinaldo got into the swing of things, donning a dark violet cloak with stiff lace at the neck. He smiled and looked more relaxed than he had when I first met him. I was beginning to warm up to him more but still secretly wished I could be alone with Gino.

We ate in our costumes. The simple meal of peas and artichokes tossed into pasta with eggs and various spices came together easily and we consumed it with some excellent white wine amid laughter and silly poses. I don't remember which of us ended up in the living room first, but the dancing began shortly thereafter.

As Gino danced with me, his face only inches from my cleavage, I began to forget that Rinaldo was in the room. We moved to the music in our heads, and when his lips grazed my breast, I had to stop myself from removing it from the dress to feed him a nipple.

His mouth sprinkled kisses on my breasts (which the dress pushed up and displayed quite nicely, I might add) and just as we came together in a long, wet, passionate kiss, I felt the back of my dress rise up to expose my panties. Rinaldo the opportunist at work.

Strangely, though, I was not disturbed by this uninvited grope. Gino's sensuality and warmth were abundant enough to make me forget that I wasn't wild about Rinaldo. My breasts were out of the dress now and being reverently manhandled by Gino. Meanwhile, Rinaldo's fingers slipped between my legs and stroked until my lips moistened. Little did he know they juiced not for him but for Gino. But who cared? We were all getting what we wanted.

Gino brought my hand to his eager but smaller-than-standard erection. There are some men who simply inspire fellatio—their cocks are pretty and shapely and just the right color. I didn't even need to look at Gino's to know that it was eminently suckable. When I took it into my mouth, my hunch was confirmed. He tasted sweet and clean and my mouth hadn't been so happy since my *malaga e meringa* gelato experience.

Bent forward to eat Gino's delicious cock, I now exposed more of myself to Rinaldo. While I sucked Gino, Rinaldo licked at my labia, tickling it before he arrived at my slit. The quiet, wet, smacking sounds filled the room and the aroma of my pussy threatened to replace the recently cooked meal.

Gino pumped my mouth. Not in a mean-spirited, "take this, bitch" kind of way, but in rhythmic, gentle motions that told me the pitch of his gradual surrender. I adored the taste of him in my mouth.

Meanwhile, Rinaldo's cock drilled its way into my cunt. At Rinaldo's first thrust, Gino extracted himself from my mouth and when I looked up at his face to find out why, he smiled and held up a finger, implying that I'd understand in a minute.

Without Gino to help maintain my balance, however, Rinaldo's ramming grew more challenging to withstand. I pressed my palms against my knees to prevent me from flying forward.

When Gino returned, Rinaldo asked him something and Gino laughed in response. *"Gradisce il gelato,"* he told him. When I saw what he held in his hand, I deduced he'd told Rinaldo "she likes gelato."

Rinaldo said something else and it sounded like scolding, but I figured most of what came out of his mouth sounded that way, so I didn't flinch. He fucked me slower as Gino spooned gelato of an unknown flavor into my waiting mouth. Did Rinaldo actually care if I liked it?

It was a flavor unknown to me. Creamy and light, its sweetness was negligible but compelling, nonetheless. The nearest I could come to guessing was dulce de leche (sweet cream) and that's what I said aloud as Rinaldo slid in and out of me.

"Nooooo," I heard from behind me. Gino smiled, raised his eyebrows, and shook his head, encouraging me to guess again.

The men exchanged more conversation and then navigated me to the sofa, where they stood before me, cocks at the ready. My dress had been removed in transit and both men had, at some point, discarded their costumes. Rather than feed me more gelato, Rinaldo put his knob to my lips. Damn if it wasn't as pretty as Gino's. I still can't recall if it tasted as good, because the gelato still resonated on my taste buds.

When Rinaldo's cock was firmly ensconced in my mouth, Gino pushed himself inside, too. I'd always dreamed of eating two cocks at once! Neither man stretched the limits of my oral capacity, so hav-ing both of them on my tongue was somewhat unwieldy but nowhere near impossible. I held one of their ass cheeks in each hand as they squirreled their meat into my mouth.

Gino pulled out a bit, spooned some gelato on his cock, and eased it back into my mouth. The creaminess mixed with somebody's pre-come but the result remained delicious. Both men gasped at the initial chill but chuckled at the inventive feeding method Gino had devised. Gino served me several more helpings of the mysterious flavor before Rinaldo erupted in my mouth and cursed himself for coming too quickly (I didn't need to know Italian to realize the import of what he muttered).

Gino then laid me back on the sofa and took me missionary style. When his cock entered my pussy, the scent of the gelato mixed briefly with the smell of sex but was soon eclipsed by it. He fucked me beautifully—it was the position I'd wanted to be in with him since I'd seen him at La Maschera. Rinaldo knelt beside me and fed me more gelato, which was so comical, I giggled, sending little rivulets of gelato down my chin.

Gino came when I did—another little piece of magic that seemed fitting for an Italian encounter—and hugged and kissed me when it was over. Rinaldo got dressed.

"So, you must tell me," I implored. "What flavor is that?"

Gino grinned and gestured toward Rinaldo. *"Panna,"* Rinaldo said, then explained in English, "Whipped cream."

"You like?" Gino asked, eyes wide with excitement.

"Oh yes!"

"It goes on sale tomorrow," Rinaldo continued. "You are the first to try."

I looked from one man to another, uncertain about the implications of Rinaldo's explanation. Gino came to my rescue.

"Rinaldo owns Vivoli!"

Well, I guess if I were responsible for the most scrumptious concoction in Italy, I'd have a healthy swagger and an inflated ego, too. I understood Rinaldo—and appreciated him—more now, and although I applauded Gino's ingenious route to a steady supply of gelato, I wished Rinaldo was just a bit more likable. I refrained from telling him the full extent of my gelato fetish. He offered to drive me to my hotel, but I declined, not wanting to risk fending him off if he wanted another round. If he was part of the package deal with Gino, I could accept that but Rinaldo solo, I didn't want, even if he came with a lifetime supply of gelato.

"Let me give you a mask to take with you," Gino said to me as he kissed me goodbye. "For you to remember me."

I adored his work, loved every mask I'd seen, but I hesitated at his offer because I knew my suitcase wouldn't accommodate another thing, especially something that required padding.

"Give her gelato," Rinaldo said, misinterpreting my hesitation as a lack of interest.

Gino laughed. "Gelato better?"

"Well, yes," I admitted, already salivating at the thought. *Panna* would be the perfect complement to the hazelnut *gianduia* I was craving. I hoped Vivoli would still be open at this hour so I could commemorate my Italian "double-header" with two scoops of gelato.

Cupcake
by Stan Kent

It had been a very liquid dinner, as are most affairs when I visit my agent, Claudia, in New York. Every time we meet, we strive for that state of perfect equilibrium—half writer, half whisky—as we discuss where next to take my smut authoring career.

It was late July and typically hot and humid. We'd begun our quest at about six with pre-prandial cocktails at a small restaurant in the Village that was crowded, hot and noisy. My girlfriend, Lizzie, had joined us, as she provides much of the inspiration for what I write, and these evenings were always more social than business. Lizzie had dressed for a New York summer night. She wore almost nothing other than sexy, strappy Jimmy Choos. Her shoulder-less dress was microscopically short and demanded no bra. If she turned too much to one side or another it was exposed nipple time. If she bent in the slightest, it was thong heaven rising.

After dinner and many drinks, we three happy souls had stumbled from bar to bar with me copping many a Lizzie feel and view until we somehow ended up in a sex shop discussing the merits of various dildos with the proprietor.

We were very drunk.

Recognizing that perhaps we had passed right on by that state of perfect equilibrium, we saw Claudia to her apartment with promises to follow-up on all the writing projects we'd discussed—if only I could remember them after the numerous toasts we'd enjoyed. Lizzie and I debated whether to go out clubbing, but decided why waste a good buzz. We'd go back to our hotel and fuck ourselves sober.

As we strolled arm-in-supportive-arm to the Meat Packing District we came upon a crowd of hipsta-kinda-people lined up outside a store at the corner of 11th and Bleecker. Both Lizzie and I checked our watches—it was after midnight. This wasn't a bar. It wasn't a restaurant. What were they doing at this hour waiting in line?

From across Bleecker Street we saw the sign—the Magnolia Bakery. Intrigued, we crossed the street and joined the line. We didn't know of the establishment's fame from *Sex and the City*. That we learned from the bubbly woman next to us in line who told us how great the cupcakes were, how much of a New York institution the place was after a night of drinking, and how Carrie and Miranda devoured cupcakes here in one episode or another. Lizzie and I looked at each other—cupcakes would indeed be a perfect way to soak up the alcohol, and we'd take a few extras back to the hotel because we'd surely be hungry later. And we did want to have sex and we were in the city, so when in New York do like a New Yorker and have cupcakes after midnight.

We joined the line, and waited for almost half-an-hour until we reached the door where a bouncer-guy with a headset was conducting crowd control. We were amazed to the point of giggling. This was a seriously hip candy spot to require rope control. Living in LA, we're used to the doorman obstacle course at all the trendy nightspots that want to appear hipper than Paris Hilton's thong, but this Magnolia place was a bakery!

There was something about being drunk that made us see the funny side of waiting in a doorman-controlled line to buy cupcakes, so we didn't bail but stood our hipster ground. As a crowd emerged, glowing with their boxes of cupcakes, we were finally granted access, and we went wild. There's something about finally making it inside that encouraged the binging, and the reason no doubt for the bakery's sign of "Limit 12 per person." It had to be all that sugar vapor doping us up as we drooled our way around the tiny space, but we bought every kind of chocolate sponge buttercream frosted cupcake the Magnolia could bake, filling up four small boxes—sixteen cupcakes at a $1.75 a pop.

What were we going to do with all that sugary softness?

Well, we ate one between us on the walk back to the Hotel Gansevoort, and that sugar bomb sure did wire our alcohol-doused bodies. Now we were really buzzed. By the time we reached our room we were beyond giggling. We were in hysterics—alcohol and cupcakes are a dangerous combination. Now we understood why so many people were standing there in line. These cupcakes were like three-inch-wide candy coated drugs, and we were fast becoming addicts.

Lizzie shimmied out of her dress and kicked off her Jimmy Choos. As she danced around naked I lost my clothes and dived on the bed. She grabbed a box and carried it over to me, balanced on her elevated palm like a fancy waiter.

"Cupcake, Cupcake?"

I had to be honest.

"I can't eat another one. I'm so full. I'll throw up if I take one more bite."

Lizzie's smile went from ear to ear.

"I'm not talking about eating them, silly."

My smile matched Lizzie's grin.

"Then I'll take two."

"Now you're talking."

Lizzie freed two chocolate buttercream cupcakes from the box.

"Close your eyes."

I did, thinking she was going to rub the tasty morsels on her breasts and then stick her creamy chocolate bosom in my face, but I was mistaken. I shuddered as the soft stickiness of the coating met my cock.

"Keep your eyes closed or I'll stop."

As much as I wanted to watch, I was more than willing to obey Lizzie's command. The feeling of chocolate frosting on my cock was a whole lot of new fun.

"I want you to imagine you're at an orgy and you're blindfolded and there are all these naked bodies around you and all of a sudden you feel this soft, creamy pussy on your cock."

All I could do was sigh. The cupcakes smashed tight between Lizzie's hands, pulsing around my cock, did feel like a luxurious pussy; the moist, spongy cake filling was just like a pussy's texture.

"She begins to fuck you, slowly at first."

Lizzie moved the cupcake pussy up and down the length of my shaft, massaging the cream and cake into my skin with her fingers. It was an incredible series of sensations from the warmth and slick stickiness of the frosting to the fluffiness of the cake manipulated by Lizzie's nimble touch. It did feel like a pussy—a damn fine one at that. I couldn't keep still. I lifted up my hips and thrusted into her chocolate coated pussy palms with a delicious sounding splat.

"Be careful!"

Lizzie was half laughing the admonition. I opened my eyes. I'd splattered the cupcake mess up her chest and onto her neck and in her hair and there were even some blobs on the bed. It was decadent the way the dark chocolate mixture coated Lizzie's soft Asian skin. She scooped a big dollop of frosting from her neck and licked it from her coated fingers.

"Yum yum. These cupcakes are too good."

I twitched my cock, sending more cupcake and frosting flying around the bed along with my not-so-subtle blowjob solicitation.

"There's plenty more if you're still hungry."

Lizzie chuckled and took another cupcake from the box, one with bright neon pink frosting. She stuck her finger in the bottom and scooped out some of the cake.

"I've always enjoyed a nice big mushroom head."

She grabbed my chocolate-coated cock and planted the pink cupcake on the crown. My erection bobbed. We laughed as it teetered. Lizzie looked around the room. Her gaze landed on our digital camera.

"I have to get a picture. Here, lick my fingers clean."

Lizzie offered me her hands and I slurped off the mess, giving her digits a good tonguing in the process. She was squirming by the time I had her hands clean enough to pick up the Nikon. Big mistake. As I mentioned, cupcakes and alcohol are a dangerous combination. Now Lizzie has pictures of an inebriated me with a pink cupcake on my chocolate-covered cock, lying spread-eagled on a chocolate-splattered bed. I'd better never piss Lizzie off, or I have a feeling my cupcake cock fame will spread across the Internet.

I couldn't help but notice that Lizzie put the camera down safely out of my reach. I would have loved to have pictures of her eating away at my bulbous pink cupcaked cock, but I'd have to settle for the memories as she steadied the slick shaft in her hands and nibbled away at the pink frosting and the cake, working her way around the head as she stroked my shaft. Accompanying her nibbling was a delightful series of slurps, moans and pronouncements of how good I tasted as she masturbated my cupcaked cock into her mouth.

Now, a Lizzie blowjob is a thing to behold, but the additional stimulus of chocolate frosting and spongy cake being devoured from my sensitized erection had me writhing and biting my chocolated fingers. Lizzie was careful to bite down softly as she bit off chunks of cupcake, nipping at my cockflesh, soothing it with her tongue as she worked the frosting onto my skin and then into her mouth. As cupcake crumbled, she caught the bits and massaged them into my balls, snaking a frosting covered finger up my ass. I had been teased and tantalized all evening from the way she dressed to now. I was on a very short fuse and the finger up my butt as she sucked down on my pink-frosted cockhead was too much. I came like a rocket, my orgasm shooting through the frosting to add an extra creaminess to Lizzie's mouthful.

"Hmmmmmm," was all Lizzie could say. Her mouth was full, and she was coming towards my face, her snowball cupcake intent more than clear to me as she left frosting handprints on the bed with each of her wicked advancements. Once directly above me, she lowered herself and French kissed me, full on depositing a messy combination of my come, pink frosting and chocolate cupcake in my mouth. Our tongues worked the batter to and fro between us as if we were beaters back at the Magnolia Bakery until it oozed out of our mouths as we pressed our lips together. We were a real mess.

One box of cupcakes down—three to go.

It is well known that eating chocolate gives an endorphin rush, and the biochemical turn-on from all the frosting and cake we'd ingested, coupled with the euphoria of being drunk and high from being in love and lust turned us into little kids with adult equipment and an abundance of gooey, fun food. We dove into the remaining boxes, grabbing handfuls of cupcakes of all frosting colors, and wrestled each other, squashing the cupcakes between us, occasionally separating to kneel on the edges of the bed, nothing but a few feet of messy bed sheets between us, hurling handfuls of frosting at each other, and all the while we couldn't stop laughing. Before we knew it, we were down to the last box, and this I wanted to make special for Lizzie. It was time to stop fooling around.

"Lie down and be still for a while."

Lizzie was still in a feisty mood, bouncing up and down on her knees.

"Why?"

"Because. Now you get your reward."

Lizzie's frosted face lit up. Her smile shone from a mess of pink, yellow, white and chocolate frosting. She looked like a messy, sexy clown.

"A foot massage. You spoil me."

"After all that walking in high heels you deserve nothing less, and we have the perfect soothing foot balm."

It's a longstanding (pun intended) pact we have between us. Lizzie indulges my love of seeing her in high heels, and in return for the pain of standing and dancing on four-inch spikes, I lavish her with hours of foot massages to ease away the discomfort. I usually have a variety of soothing lotions and creams, but tonight there would be no need for those. Tonight Lizzie was going for a walk in the cupcakes.

I elevated Lizzie's feet by putting a couple of pillows under her legs. I took a cupcake in each hand and pressed them into Lizzie's soles. She shuddered.

"That feels so good. From now on we always use frosting for foot massages. We should market it. We'd make a fortune."

"Relax. Enjoy your foot massage."

"I can't. I'm wired from all the sugar. My brain is zooming."

Lizzie had a point. There was no way we were going to come down, so I put all that energy into kneading Lizzie's feet. I squeezed the frosting and cake between her toes and worked the excess into all the pressure points as if I were trying to burrow inside her body, and then I started licking the mess from each toe, starting with the littlest, going up to the biggest and back down to the littlest, like I was playing one of those Pan pipes. This had Lizzie writhing, giggling hysterically, clutching her stomach as if she had to pee. I sucked each toe as if it were a little chocolate dick. I held her ankles tightly while I gave her another toe-sucking cycle, but my hands were slippery from the frosting and she broke free. She was a woman possessed by cupcakes. She pushed me down and straddled my frosted cock, sinking its sugary length inside her in one swift movement. I propped myself up on my arms and sucked on her frosted nipples, licking the coating from them with my tongue.

Lizzie's body was sensitized from too much sugar. My tongue's touch on her nipples drove her into a frenzy. She pushed me down to the bed, reached into the box, grabbed a cupcake and smashed it between her legs, pulping it between us as she pounded her frosted clit on my chocolaty body. At this point I was just along for the ride, doing my best to hold on as Lizzie funneled a most unusual evening of sex and cupcakes into a single-minded rush to come. She bounced up and down, clutching at her breasts, pulling on her nipples as we both felt the squelch of the crushed cupcake between our sliding genitals. She grabbed my coated fingers and stuffed them into her mouth, and as she came she stifled the usual laugh that she gives off by sucking and biting on my candied hands.

She collapsed forward, and I held her tightly, my cock twitching inside her chocolate box. We stayed like that for an hour or more, picking tasty bits from our bodies until the sleep of the well-fucked claimed us.

We didn't have hangovers the next day. All that sugar must have combated the alcohol. The room was a mess, which we did our best to clean up. The worst of it was confined to the bed sheets, which could be cleaned. We had to wipe a few mirrors and walls down, but at least we hadn't destroyed anything. As we cleansed ourselves in the shower we agreed it was the most fun we'd had with our clothes off in a long time, and we do have a lot of such naked fun, regularly, but the addition of the cupcakes as sex toys had really turned up the heat in the most unexpected of ways. We'd have never thought to buy buttercream frosted chocolate cupcakes and smear them all over our bodies and into various orifices for foreplay, duringplay and afterplay.

And we still had one left for breakfast.

Or maybe . . .

About the Authors

L. Elise Bland has always lived her life in the fast lane. She has worked as a stripper, a dominatrix, a fetish model, a sex educator, and an actress in erotic films. Along the way, she started writing erotica inspired by her adventures. Her most recent publications include *Naughty Spanking Stories from A to Z 2* (Pretty Things Press) and *The Best American Erotica 2006* (Fireside / Touchstone.) In her free time, Elise indulges in exotic European cheeses and practices the fine art of Middle Eastern dance. Learn more about her writings at www.lelisebland.com.

Cheyenne Blue combines her two passions in life and writes travel guides and erotica. Her erotica has appeared in several anthologies, including *Best Women's Erotica, Mammoth Best New Erotica, Best Lesbian Erotica, Best Lesbian Love Stories*, and on many websites. Her travel guides have been jammed into many glove boxes underneath the chocolate wrappers. You can see more of her erotica on her web site, www.cheyenneblue.com.

Tenille Brown's fiction is featured online and in several print anthologies including *Naughty Spanking Stories From A to Z, Santa's Sweets* and *Amazons: Sexy Tales Of Strong Women, Glamour Girls: Femme/Femme Erotica* and *Midnight Confessions*. She keeps a daily blog at: http:/ /thesteppingstone.blogspot.com and a website, www.tenillebrown.com.

Jennifer Dziura is a comedian best known for orchestrating the Williamsburg Spelling Bee, an adult spelling bee in Brooklyn for which she landed on the front page of the *New York Times* Style section. She has had fiction published in the *Powhatan Review* and *Monkeybicycle,* and for several years wrote a humor column in a regional newspaper for which she won a National Society of Newspaper Columnists award in humor writing (followed by brief careers in dotcom entrepreneurship and lingerie modeling, in that order). Jennifer writes a daily comedy blog at www.jenisfamous.com, and satirically reviews sex toys at www.sarcasticsex.com.

R. Gay is a writer who has always wanted to work for a traveling carnival. Her work can be found in numerous anthologies including *Best American Erotica 2004*, *Binary: Best of Both Worlds*, *Sweet Life*, and *A Is for Amour* among others.

Shanna Germain is a connoisseur of anything that can be put in her mouth: dark chocolate, oatmeal stouts, single-origin coffees, various body parts, silky fabrics, and nasturtiums. You can read her work, erotic and otherwise, in *Aqua Erotica*, *Best American Erotica 2007*, *Best Bondage Erotica 2*, *Slave to Love* and on her website, www.shannagermain.com.

Sacchi Green writes in western Massachusetts and the mountains of New Hampshire. Her work has appeared in *Best of Best Lesbian Erotica 2*, *Best of Best Women's Erotica*, *Penthouse*, *Naughty Spanking Stories from A to Z*, and a thigh-high stack of other anthologies with inspirational covers. She co-edited *Rode Hard, Put Away Wet: Lesbian Cowboy Erotica* with Rakelle Valencia, and their second anthology, *Hard Road, Easy Riding: Lesbian Biker Erotica* was published in the fall of 2006.

Michelle Houston has stories in *Heat Wave*, *Naughty Spanking Stories From A to Z volumes 1 & 2*, *Three-way*, and *The Merry XXXmas Book of Erotica*, as well as several other anthologies. You can see more about her writings on her personal website, The Erotic Pen (www.eroticpen.net).

Jolene Hui is a writer/actor who loves to watch TV, eat sweets, and dream of the day when she will get her Chinese Crested Hairless and Standard Poodle so that she can finally have the family she always desired.

Bianca James is a multilingual genderfluid writer living in Berkeley and Chicago. Her stories have appeared in anthologies such as *Best American Erotica 2006* and *Best of the Best Meat Erotica*. Most of her dirty stories seem to involve food as well as sex.

Stan Kent is a chameleon hair colored former nightclub owning rocket scientist author of erotic novels. Stan has penned nine original, unique and very naughty works including the *Shoe Leather* series. Selections from his books have been featured in the *Best of Erotic Writing Blue Moon* collections. Stan has hosted an erotic talk show night at Hustler Hollywood for the last five years. *The Los Angeles Times* described his monthly performances as "combination moderator and lion tamer." To see samples of his works and his latest hair colors, visit Stan at www.StanKent.com or email him at stan@stankent.com.

Tsaurah Litzky believes that eating candy is the next best thing to sex, and when she can combine the two, she is truly blessed, so she particularly enjoyed writing this story for *Sex and Candy*. Her erotica has appeared in many publications including *Best American Erotica*, *Penthouse*, *The Blacklisted Journalist*, *Politically Inspired*, *The Williamsburg Observer*, *Clean Sheets*, *Naughty Spanking Stories from A to Z* and *Dare*. Her erotic novella, *The Motion of the Ocean*, is included in *Three the Hard Way*, a series of erotic novellas edited by Susie Bright and published by Simon & Schuster. She teaches erotic writing at The New School and erotic poetry at the Bowery Poetry Club.

Catherine Lundoff is a professional computer geek and transplanted Brooklynite who lives in Minneapolis with her fabulous partner. Her short stories have appeared in such anthologies as *Stirring Up a Storm*, *Naughty Spanking Stories from A to Z*, *Hot Women's Erotica*, *Blood Surrender*, *Ultimate Lesbian Erotica 2006*, *The Mammoth Book of Best New Erotica 4* and *Best Lesbian Erotica 2006*. Torquere Press released a collection of her lesbian erotica, *Night's Kiss*, in 2005 and she has a bimonthly writing column called "Nuts and Bolts" at the Erotica Readers and Writers Association (www.erotica-readers.com).

Radclyffe has written numerous best-selling lesbian romances (*Safe Harbor* and its sequels *Beyond the Breakwater* and *Distant Shores, Silent Thunder; Innocent Hearts, Love's Melody Lost, Love's Tender Warriors, Tomorrow's Promise, Passion's Bright Fury, Love's Masquerade, shadowland,* and *Fated Love*), as well as two romance/intrigue series: the Honor series (*Above All, Honor; Honor Bound; Love & Honor;* and *Honor Guards*) and the Justice series (*Shield of Justice,* the prequel *A Matter of Trust, In Pursuit of Justice, Justice in the Shadows,* and *Justice Served*). Her other works include *Stolen Moments: Erotic Interludes 2* (ed. with Stacia Seaman), *Honor Reclaimed, Turn Back Time,* and *Promising Hearts.* She also has a selection in the anthologies *Call of the Dark* and *The Perfect Valentine* from Bella Books and *First-Timers* from Alyson Books (2006). She is the president of Bold Strokes Books, a lesbian publishing company, and in 2005, retired from the practice of surgery to write and publish full-time. In addition to writing, she collects lesbian pulps, enjoys photographing scenes for her book covers, and shares her life with her partner, Lee, and assorted canines. She lives in Philadelphia, PA.

The Femmepress **Shar Rednour**, author of *The Femme's Guide to the Universe,* is also the director and co-producer of *Healing Sex* featuring Staci Haines, which helps us heal intimacy with ourselves and others after surviving abuse or trauma. This revolutionary project helps heal the world so everyone can enjoy her company's other endeavors like *Hard Love & How to Fuck In High Heels, Talk to Me Baby,* or *Bend Over Boyfriend 2: More Rockin Less Talkin.* Her short stories can be found in fabulous books. She is also a mother and wife.

Dominic Santi is a former technical editor turned rogue whose stories have appeared in many dozens of anthologies and magazines, including *Best American Erotica 2004, Best of Best Gay Erotica 2, Freshmen: The Best, His Underwear,* and many volumes of *Friction.* Santi is a firm believer in meticulous research and is extremely fond of peppermint sticks. Visit his website at www.nicksantistories.com.

Donna George Storey makes Venetians and Danish rice pudding every year at Christmas, and they're definitely worth the effort. Her fiction has appeared in *Clean Sheets*, *Taboo: Forbidden Fantasies for Couples*, *Foreign Affairs: Erotic Travel Tales*, *Mammoth Book of Best New Erotica 4* and *5*, *Best Women's Erotica 2005* and *2006* and *Best American Erotica 2006*. Read more of her work at www.DonnaGeorgeStorey.com.

S. Lynn Taylor lives on Tampa Bay, with her beautiful muse of twenty-five years, and their "boys"–Spookie Mulder, a lazy black cat and Poochini Buffington, a sweet but neurotic Bichon. She writes horror and sci-fi, but recently took a class taught by Catherine Lundoff and discovered she also loves writing smut.

Sage Vivant operates Custom Erotica Source (www.customeroticasource.com), where she and her staff of writers create tailor-made erotic fiction for individual clients. With partner M. Christian, she has edited *Confessions: Admissions of Sexual Guilt; Amazons; Garden of the Perverse; Leather, Lace and Lust;* and *The Best of Both Worlds: Bisexual Erotica*. She is the author of the novel *Giving the Bride Away.* Her short stories have appeared in dozens of anthologies, including *American Casanova, Stirring Up A Storm,* and *The Mammoth Book of Best New Erotica*. Listen to her podcasts at http://sage.libsyn.com.

Salome Wilde is the pen name of an academic enjoying her midlife crisis by writing erotica. Her work has been published in such venues as *Clean Sheets* and Susie Bright's *Best American Erotica 2006*, and she is currently at work on a BDSM novel. Visit her at www.salomewilde.com.

SékouWrites is a New York based writer and relationship columnist. He is the editor of the serial novel *When Butterflies Kiss* and serves as Managing Editor of *UPTOWN* magazine. Find out more at www.sekouwrites.com.

Writer, voyeur, and provocateur, **Michele Zipp**'s oral fixations also extend to the aural. Her articles on sex and relationships have been featured in *Playgirl* magazine, where she was editor-in-chief for many years. Her erotica writing can be found in *Naughty Stories From A to Z 1* and *3*, *Heat Wave*, *Juicy Erotica*, *Naughty Spanking Stories From A to Z 1* and *2*, and *Best Bondage Erotica*. She is currently the Editor of New York Moves magazine. And of course, she is sucking on a red lollipop right now.

About the Editor

Rachel Kramer Bussel is a professional smutmonger. She serves as Senior Editor at *Penthouse Variations*, and hosts the monthly In The Flesh Erotic Reading Series in New York City. Her books include *Naughty Spanking Stories from A to Z 1* and *2*, *Up All Night*, *First-Timers*, *Glamour Girls: Femme/Femme Erotica*, *Ultimate Undies: Erotic Stories about Underwear and Lingerie*, *Sexiest Soles: Erotic Stories about Feet and Shoes*, *Secret Slaves: Erotic Stories of Bondage,* and, with Alison Tyler, *Caught Looking: Erotic Tales of Voyeurs and Exhibitionists* and *Hide and Seek.* Her smutty tales have been published in over 100 anthologies, including *Best American Erotica 2004* and *2006*, *Best Women's Erotica 2003, 2004,* and *2006, Juicy Erotica,* and others. She conducts interviews for Gothamist.com and Mediabistro.com, and has written for Alternative Press, *AVN, Bust,* Cleansheets.com, *Curve, Diva, Girlfriends, Metro, On Our Backs,* Oxygen.com, *Penthouse, Penthouse Forum, Playgirl, Zink,* and other publications. Rachel has appeared on Showtime's Family Business, The Berman and Berman Show (Discovery Health), and Naked New York. She likes sugar any way she can get it, but is most passionate about cupcakes, and has the blog to prove it at http://cupcakestakethecake.blogspot.com. For anything else you want to know, visit www.rachelkramerbussel.com

Pretty Things Press, Inc.

www.prettythingspress.com

Naughty Stories
from A to Z

Spanking Stories
from A to Z

Spanking Stories
from A to Z, Volume 2

Juicy Erotica

Naughty Stories
from A to Z, Volume 2

30 Erotic Stories
Written Just for Him

30 Erotic Stories
Written Just for Her

Naked Erotica

Naughty Stories
from A to Z, Volume 3

Down and Dirty

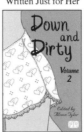

Down and Dirty,
Volume 2

Bad Girl

Naughty Stories
from A to Z, Volume 4

Velvet Heat

Sex & Candy

Sex & Coffee